AF444525

A New Broom

A fantasy for children of all ages

By

David Connolly

© David Connolly 2006

The moral right of the author has been asserted.

All rights reserved.

No part of this publication may be reproduced, stored in a retrieval system, or transmitted in any form or by any means, without the prior permission in writing of the publisher, nor be otherwise circulated in any form of binding or cover other than that in which it is published and without a similar condition including this condition being imposed on the subsequent purchaser.

Thrillers by the author include

Freeman
Hardy
Willis
(A Trilogy)

The Legacy of Harry Dean
The Ghost of Thomas Reed
The Death of Adam Semple
Insider
Life Support
The Specialist
The Norfolk Sanction
Breakdown
Vendetta
The Arlington Network

Shakespeare's Monkey
(Science Fiction)

For Diana, Sarah, Abigail and Matthew who
encouraged me when I needed it most

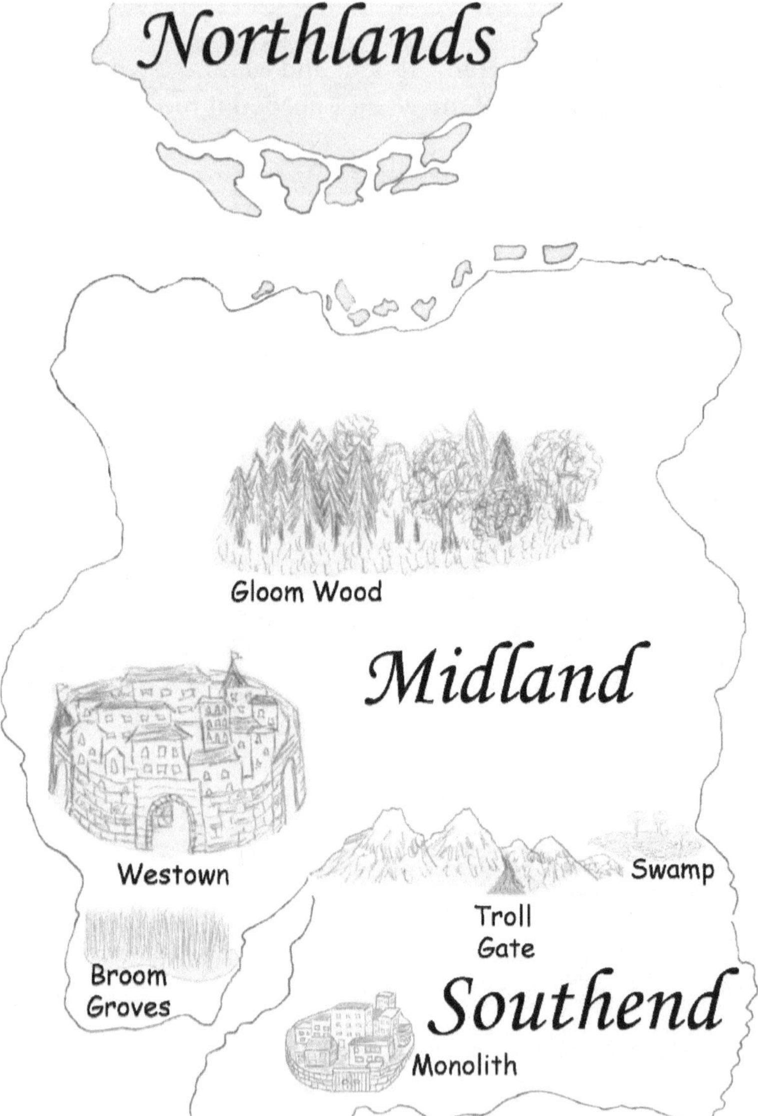

Northlands
Gloom Wood
Midland
Westown
Broom
Groves
Troll
Gate
Swamp
Southend
Monolith

The Voting

It was an odd, ill assorted group which sat round the camp fire. Most of them were wearing cloaks of dark hue and the general greyness was brightened only when the firelight caught the brightly coloured breeches and jerkins which they wore beneath. There was a general chatter, which ebbed and flowed for half an hour as a few more individuals arrived and were either greeted noisily or allowed to seat themselves in silence. As the group grew in size and diversity the fire grew brighter. Some had been drinking and wanted to sing while others were impatient to leave. One tall fellow who wanted to do both had stood up several times only to be pulled down again by his companions. Another short thickset character with a long salt and pepper beard had also tried to stand but had fallen over every time.

Both the group and the fire were well concealed from all directions by virtue of their position inside a ring of oak trees which nestled in a hollow. Once or twice the almost full moon had peeped silently out from the clouds, but even by full moonlight the scene had an eerie greyness about it.

Suddenly the fire flared up and cast its bright glow over everybody circled around it. The noise and chatter subsided and there was an air of expectancy in the place. People cast their eyes hither and yon looking for something to happen. Without a sound or any flash of light a figure was suddenly standing in the centre of the group. He was tall and the effect of his height was enhanced by the high pointed hat he wore. He was covered by a cloak which almost reached the ground and supported himself with a staff. He spoke with a deep clear voice.

"My friends, you are all aware, to some degree, of the general reason for our meeting here, but some of you will not know, or like, the suggestion which has been put forward." He paused to let the opening remarks sink in. "The trolls in the Southland are, once again, on the rampage and once again we are faced with the problem of keeping our families and possessions from them. The unusual feature of this occasion is that they are rumoured to be using dragons to lead their attack."

The last piece of information brought forth a few gasps and a general buzz of discontent. When this had died down the tall man carried on. "In the past we have beaten the trolls comfortably, but this particular year, after a bad harvest and with many of our young men leaving for more prosperous regions, we may have difficulty. Rather than use up all our resources straight away in an effort which will, at best, only keep the trolls quiet for hundred years or so, several groups have suggested that we try to put a stop to their actions forever. To do this we need help and that will have to be paid for. The proposal which is being put to lodges everywhere tonight is the same; that we hire a sorcerer."

The last word sent a shudder through the whole crowd. The tall chap who had tried to leave stood up and addressed the assembly.

"Who's going to pay for a sorcerer? ... Eh? They always want gold and we haven't got much left these days. And who's going to deal with him? Have you thought of that? They're tricky those sorcerers and it's certain that none of the elves will want to deal with one ….."

"Typical elven rubbish," shouted the short man who had done all the falling over earlier on. "Miss the point. Ask the wrong questions and evade any responsibility. Dealing with a sorcerer is no problem. I or any other dwarf could manage that. The problem is how do we contact one? They don't walk down the road looking for contracts. Also you can't guarantee what you get. I recall that the pixies hired one and he refused to do anything without payment in advance…. And when he'd been paid he just worked a few quick spells and pushed off. No! What we need is some sort of guarantee of results."

"Don't be more foolish than you have to," said the tall elf, "We're talking about sorcerers, not second hand broom dealers. They don't give guarantees to anybody. Least of all dwarves."

The dwarf, who had fallen over again in the meantime, struggled back to his feet.

"Well at least we can try some tough negotiating. You elves would let him get away with anything. And nobody's yet said where we're going to get one. What about it Axel ?"

The original speaker stood up again.

"There are people who remember the incantations and the conditions required to call up a sorcerer. All we need is agreement in principle and we'll get on with the preparations. We also need somebody from each of the sects to negotiate. I'll stand for the Wizards, who will stand for the dwarves and the elves?"

"I'll stand for the dwarves." said the short thickset falling down speaker. "I, Bandor, will negotiate with sorcerers. Who will stand for the elves?" There was no reply.

"Come on, one of you must have some courage."
Silence
"Surely you're not all afraid"
There was a pause and then from the rear of a small group of elves at the outer edge of the ring, came a small voice
"I'll try if there's nobody else"
There was nobody else and the owner of the small voice was quickly thrust forward.

"Who is it?" everyone asked, particularly the elves.

"I'm Leander and I've seen trolls and dragons before and I can't think of anything more frightening than they are, not even sorcerers."

"Praise be for an elf with some guts," said Bandor.

"That's not fair Bandor. We elves are peace loving and quiet. We don't go around fighting for fun like you do. Anyway, if I'm the only elf who's seen a dragon at close quarters then I'm the only one qualified to take the decision."

Bandor didn't understand the comment but before he could reply Axel spoke. "All that's left now is to record the vote. How many for? Please show your staffs."

The vote was taken and carried with only a few dissenters among the elves and thus it was decided to hire a sorcerer. Axel packed up his staff, wound his cloak about him and disappeared. One by one the dwarves and elves left, soundlessly, like so many candles burning out, until within two or three minutes the clearing was empty with only the dying remains of the fire to show there had ever been anybody there.

The Sorcerer

Michael O'Reilly approached the administration block of the Octel Engineering and Construction Corporation's Thunder Bay project office. He was in a black mood and quite prepared to remove anyone who stood in his way. The offices were a row of wooden huts standing knee high off the ground on steel legs. The whole building shook as he mounted the steps to the hut marked Project Manager and threw the door open. The wooden hut vibrated as he entered and slammed the door. A girl sitting behind a desk facing him said " Yes Mr. O'Reilly, What can I do for you?"

"Nothing," he said and strode past her leaving her open mouthed. He kicked the door behind her which was marked 'M. Sprenzel - Consultant Engineer'. It opened and O'Reilly walked in.

" Sprenzel," he shouted "You'd better just sit there and keep your mouth shut because if you open it I'm just likely to fill it with my size nine, specially toughened, steel toe-capped boot." He paused momentarily for breath: "Since I've been on this job you've scrapped perfectly good steel structures, used the wrong grades of material and upset the workforce. Each time I've got you out of trouble. But not satisfied with holding up the job and overspending, this morning you struck the shuttering on one of my concrete sections before it was ready and the whole thing collapsed. You're an incompetent, dangerous fool and I wouldn't employ you to repair my garden shed, let alone build a something as complex as a dam. I'm quitting before people start to think I'm responsible for your mistakes"

"O'Reilly, you can't talk to me........"

That was the last Mike heard from Sprenzel as he closed the door with force enough to rattle the whole building again.

The relief he felt after quitting was mildly marred by the question of what he was going to do next. He had enough cash to last about three months and was fed up with the Canadian cold. He decided to head toward the East Coast and turn south when the fancy took him. He knew some people back in the U.S. who might give him a job and, if the worst came to the worst he could always get a plane to London or Shannon and stay with one of his six older brothers until he found a job. He squeezed his six foot, one hundred and seventy pound frame behind the wheel of his beaten up Land Rover and drove back to base camp. He picked up all his gear, apart from two cans of beer, which he left for his successor, and began his journey east.

Within a couple of days he was driving through the warmer atmosphere of the New England springtime. Apart from moving generally south the weather had improved and Mike was feeling good. The air was cold but the sun was warm and the whole world seemed to be peaceful. Mike was driving at a steady fifty miles per hour along a two lane blacktop road thinking of the next job he would like to do and the next girl he would like to meet. The road moved hypnotically down the windscreen with the next bit looking just like the last. It had been that way for the last four hours. So much so that it was almost a relief when the huge oak tree suddenly appeared about a fifty yards in front of the Rover.

Mike's brain did not register what was wrong but his foot did. He pressed firmly on the brake and found the Land Rover sliding and bumping over grass and mud toward the tree.

Another ten feet and he would have made it. As it was he hit the tree with a sickening thump which put his mind slightly out of focus and another small dent in the Rover. He climbed out and stood beside the tree rubbing his head and cursing mildly. He looked carefully but could see no sign of the road, just green grass and skid marks in the warm sunshine. He looked again at the tree and saw, peeping out from behind it, the face of a man.

"For heaven's sake come out from there and tell me what happened. Where's the road?"

The face stepped out and Mike saw that it was attached to a tall willowy man wearing a long black cloak and a pointed hat.

"Good afternoon sir," the man said, "My name is Axel. Would you be kind enough to tell me whom I am addressing?"

"I'm Mike O'Reilly but where I am I do not know."

"Praise be. You are a sorcerer. Only a sorcerer would have a mystical name like Miko"

"Sorcerer? I'm an engineer. But what on earth are you?"

"As I said my name is Axel. Permit me to introduce my companions," Axel beckoned and out from behind the tree came a group of people. There was a short thickset man called Bandor. He stood about four feet six inches, carried a staff and had an axe in his belt. There was a tall, skinny nervous one named Leander who carried a staff as though it were made of gelignite. There was a fat, red-faced man of medium height who wore red trousers, green jacket and yellow hat. His beard was white, and instead of a staff be carried a fishing rod. His name was Irving. There was a pale thin girl who seemed to be almost transparent, who's name was Lutetia, and one who looked like a daisy and was named Pallisy. There was a tall, raven haired, athletic looking woman wearing a red sequined leotard and black fishnet tights beneath a green satin cloak. Her name was Esmeralda. And finally there was a little man dressed entirely in green whose name was Wilberforce.

Mike looked at the collection before him and pinched himself, convinced he was suffering a concussion. When Axel had introduced each of them he said to the group

"This is our sorcerer. His name is Miko."

This started a buzz of conversation as the negotiating committee, for such it was, all tried to ask different questions at once. It was more than Mike could stand.

"Hold it!" he bellowed. The response was instantaneous. Half the group disappeared leaving Axel, Bandor, Esmeralda and the one with the fishing rod, whose name Mike had already forgotten. When the silence was re-established the heads of the missing members of the party reappeared from behind the tree and they came out again whispering apologetically.

"Firstly, I am not a sorcerer," said Mike, "and secondly, where am I?"

Axel consulted a large book which he produced from under his cloak. Mike couldn't see how he could keep it there without it showing but Axel seemed to manage it easily.

"Here it is." said Axel reading from the book, "Sorcerers always deny that they are sorcerers and claim to be something else. Normally chemists, engineers or physicists, although the book does record an accountant and a lawyer, but these are specialised branches of sorcery. Er...What did you say you were Miko?

"I'm an engineer and I've gone round the twist. I'm seeing leprechauns.

"No." said Axel, consulting the book again, "the leprechauns voted against the idea and refused to send a negotiator." He continued to consult his tome for a moment and then exclaimed, "Here it is!"

"What?' chorused Mike and the rest of the group.

"It says here, and I quote, 'Traditionally sorcerers tend to deny all knowledge of their art. This is thought to be due to their need to protect their secrets. When making initial contact it is often necessary to convince the sorcerer that you know something of his abilities. In the past such magical incantations as 'leverage' or 'Gunpowder' have proved effective in opening negotiations."

As soon as Axel had said this, Bandor Esmeralda and Wilberforce started shouting,

"Leverage, Leverage, Leverage." and the rest of the group chanted

"Gunpowder, Gunpowder, Gunpowder."

Mike shook his head, still unable to make any sense of the situation.

"Okay," he said, "I'll play your games, at least until I regain my senses. What about leverage and gunpowder?"

When he said this, the group began to jump with glee." He knows, it works. Ask him what he wants." they all shouted although Mike heard only their squeals of delight.

"Now," said Axel, "We are empowered to offer you the sum of one pound of gold for each day you spend with us, subject, of course, to a demonstration of your powers."

"Ah'" Mike thought, "I'm dreaming. Just as they are about to give me the gold I'll wake up. Good."

"I accept", he said, in a loud sonorous voice, "How would you like me to demonstrate my powers?"

Axel answered in tones at least as impressive as Mike's. "We would like you to light a fire, here, beside the tree."

Mike smiled as he searched around for some twigs and leaves and arranged them in a neat pile ready for lighting, then he selected a few larger pieces of wood and put them on one side. He went to one of the bags in the back of the Land Rover and eventually he produced a four inch magnifying glass. With the aid of the sun he ignited the small pile of twigs and then added the larger pieces of wood. Within five minutes he had a very respectable blaze going.

"Amazing. Incredible. I saw it and I don't believe it." said some of the others

"How would you light a fire then?" asked Mike.

"Like this." said Axel. He snapped his fingers and another small fire appeared beside Mike's.

"Or this." Said Esmeralda, and a bolt of lightning struck the ground by Mike's feet and a circle of fire appeared. Mike stepped nimbly out of the circle and re-examined the evidence of his own eyes. The three fires and the group convinced him that he was delirious. The tree and the rest of the scenery made him sure that he wasn't.

"Okay," he said. "I said I would play, and I will. If you can make fire like that, why did you ask me to?"

Everybody was silent. Pallisy and Lutetia looked nervously at each other while Leander and Irving Looked embarrassed. Eventually Bandor spoke,

"I knew it. I knew something like this would happen. We've got a mentally retarded sorcerer."

"Wait a moment," said Axel, "let me look in the book." Once again he produced the huge volume and began to leaf through it furiously. Eventually he came to a page which caused him to stop, "Here's something...It says sorcerers are usually both ingenious and ingenuous ur ..um...blah blah blah.... not to be taken literally...umph umph umph umph..and '*it may be necessary to explain the obvious*.' This is thought to be because they need to hide their exceptionally acute perceptiveness." He closed the book and said "There, what about that?"

"I dunno," said Mike. "All I understood was blah blah and umph umph"

"Ah Miko," said Axel, You can't get away with it you know. We'll explain everything in terms a three-year-old could understand if it helps you to cover your secrets. After all, we've had a demonstration of your powers."

"You have?" said Mike quizzically.

"Yes," said Bandor, trying hard to look influential, "That fire trick was pretty terrific. Especially for a sorcerer with an I.Q. as low as yours seems to be." All the others nodded sagely at this comment. They were recovering from their fright and were beginning to admire Bandor for the way he treated the sorcerer.

"Good," said Mike. "Now perhaps you will tell me why you asked me to make a fire when you can do it so easily."

"Ah Miko," said Esmeralda, speaking at length for the first time, "We can do it because we're highly trained. After all, any graduate pyrocrat could do that. But it costs a great deal to educate graduates and still only three out of every hundred of our population get to university. Of these, only one in ten will do some type of pyrotechnics course. Axel here did his first degree in levitation and couldn't use fire at all until he returned to do a couple of years research. With your magic apparatus it appears that anybody can start a fire. Ergo, you show us how to make the apparatus and if it is cheaper than a university education, then we'll produce them."

Mike had difficulty following everything she said as he was too busy watching her face as she spoke. 'If I'm delirious,' he thought, 'you are the prettiest dream I've had for some time.' Leander interrupted his train of thought.

"Er... Do you think, now that we have established contact, we could move to a safer place. We are, after all, rather exposed here."

"Who's exposed?" asked Esmeralda, pulling her cloak tightly round her.

"Confounded elves, always worrying. Still I suppose you're right," said Bandor. "We might as well get back to the school."

Everybody agreed and nodded their heads vigorously, then, in the twinkling of an eye, they all disappeared, leaving Mike alone with the Rover and the remains of three fires.

Mike shook his head and sat down with his back resting against the front wheel of the Rover. It was madness but none-the-less he could see no trace of the road, he could see three fires burning and he could still see Esmeralda in his mind's eye. He considered the possibility that he had fallen asleep at the wheel and crashed. In that case the best thing to do would be sleep. Then he would probably wake up in hospital. He made himself comfortable facing the afternoon sun and closed his eyes. He was just drifting off into a pleasant doze when he was rudely awakened by a stabbing pain in his left side.

"Wassup" Mike gasped in sleepy surprise and put his hand out to grasp whatever it was that was stabbing him. His hand closed round somebody's wrist and held it firm until he could focus his eyes on it. As he squeezed somebody screamed and Mike found himself holding Esmeralda's ankle with the pointed toe of what looked like a glass slipper digging into his ribs.

"You're very lucky," she said, "If you weren't a valuable sorcerer I'd have burned you up for that."

"For what? What do you expect if you go around prodding people in the ribs with your boot?"

"That is not a boot. It's a very fashionable and expensive shoe. It took me ages to find them. Anyway, that's beside the point. Axel sent me to ask why you didn't come with us."

"Mainly because I don't know how or where you all went."

"We told you. We went to the school."

"Which school?"

"Why... The Western School of Philosophy of course."

"Of course. But where is it?"

"It's in Westown."

"And how do I get to Westown?"

"The normal way. Surely even sorcerers study basic kinetics."

"If you mean surely I can do that trick you all just did - No, I can't"

"Well how else do you suggest that we get there? It's far too far to walk. That's why we had to have all guildsmen to meet you. Nobody comes this far from civilization by any other means and the ordinary folk can't do it."

"Well nor can I. So how do we get there?"

Esmeralda's voice trembled. Her lips were quivering and her eyes felt prickly. "Well don't just lie there holding my ankle. Do something. I can't get all your stuff and us back to the school. In fact I'm too tired to get myself back comfortably." Then she burst into tears

Mike let go of her ankle and sprang up from the ground. He put his arm around her and made some soothing noises. When she had stopped sobbing he said, "Alright, I might be able to do something for us but I shall need some help."

Esmeralda brightened visibly when she heard this. Mike went to the Rover and took out a jerry can full of petrol. He poured a little of onto his hand and showed it to Esmeralda.

"I'll need a supply of this."

She looked at it and placed some on her fingers where it suddenly burst into flame. "That's no problem. How much do you need?" Mike showed her the petrol tank and the Jerry cans, which she filled with something close enough to petrol for the Land Rover to run. He helped her into the passenger seat and asked which way she would go if they were walking to Westown. He put the Rover into gear and moved off. Once they were underway Esmeralda snuggled up against him as best she could on the Rover's front seat.

"Miko," she said, "I had serious reservations about you in the beginning but I'm only just beginning to understand what a clever lot you sorcerers are. After all, who else would have thought of a having a set of tools which also acts as a transporter, and even though the ride is a bit lumpy, the seats are much more comfortable than sitting on a broom."

Mike thought about explaining the Rover, or asking about brooms, but he was so comfortable with her resting against him that he just continued to drive into the purple sunset.

The Forest

After about half an hour of driving Esmeralda was fast asleep and Mike was beginning to worry. He had no idea how far it was to Westown and he couldn't be completely sure that he was still going in the right direction. His fears were heightened when he found the track he was driving down disappeared into an impenetrable wood. He had no choice but to wake his companion. As soon as she awoke Mike was sorry he had disturbed her. She looked at the forest and said

"I haven't the slightest idea where we are but I do feel rested enough to go back to the school and send one of the others out to guide you in."

Then she disappeared. Mike sat at the wheel of the Rover for about twenty minutes before, without any warning, Wilberforce appeared beside him.

"We haven't been properly introduced Miko, and I know that a powerful sorcerer like yourself doesn't have much time for social niceties, but I'm Wilberforce and I'm a gremlin."

"A gremlin," laughed Mike "But you can't be, gremlins are imaginary and they cause all sorts of problems."

"That's just the sort of rumour the faeries like to spread. We do exist you know. It's just that we're frightfully clumsy and, some say, unlucky. I know a lot of sorcerers claim that some of their spell won't work because we are about."

"Okay Wilber, oh, you don't mind if I call you that? Good. I'll accept that you're a gremlin if you can tell how to get to Westown from here."

"Well you'll never get this mobile workshop of yours through these bushes so we'd better find a wider path into the forest." Wilberforce thought for a moment and then said, "If you turn left and continue for half a league or so you should come to a much wider path which you can take. Mike turned the wheel of the Rover and began to follow the gremlins instructions.

How come you know the country so well Wilber ?" he asked

"Oh, I don't, but as I told you, we gremlins are very unlucky and were it not for our one saving grace we'd probably have died out long ago. You see, our clumsiness is offset by one fact; we can always find our way home. From anywhere, under more or less any circumstances. I bet you never heard of anybody losing a gremlin."

Mike had to say that he had not but he could not bring himself to say that he did not believe in the existence of gremlins. Sure enough, after driving for about a mile and a half Mike came across a path, about seven feet wide, which led straight into the forest. He turned onto it and began to penetrate the woods.

The sinking sun had been giving less and less light as they had been driving around the periphery of the forest and as soon as they were in the body of the wood there was no natural light at all. Mike switched on the Rover's headlights but without white lines or markers he had great difficulty in seeing the track.

They drove in silence for about an hour. By this time Mike was seeing things and was worried about driving into a tree. He mentioned to Wilber that they ought to stop, at least for a while, until Mike's eyes had rested.

"WHAT?" said Wilberforce…"Stop?? In the forest?? Here?? In Gloom Wood?? You must either be very powerful or Bandor was right, You're a loony sorcerer."

"What do you mean? Why shouldn't we stop in the forest?"

"Because of the Banshee, not to mention all the other little nasties that infest these places after dark."

"Wait a minute," said Mike, his exasperation setting in again, "Are you telling me that there's a banshee and sundry other bogey men in this wood after dark?

"Of course there are. Where else would you expect them all to live?" Mike thought for a moment but kept on driving. It was becoming obvious that Wilber had only let them drive into the wood because he felt sure that a sorcerer could handle the terrors that would have normal men staying away in droves. He thought of turning round and going back but he was not up to another hour or more of driving to get back out of the dark woods.

"Ah well," he said, pulling the Land Rover to a halt. "If I can't stand up to a banshee and a couple of lesser uglybugs then you're right, I'm not much of a sorcerer." He pulled the Rover to the side of the path so there was room to lie full length beside it, and rummaged in the back for his sleeping bag. Wilberforce looked on in wonder

"How is it," he asked in a whisper, "That you will keep the banshee from taking your soul?"

"Its easy," said Mike, exasperation wearing his temper very thin, "I don't have one so he can't take it."

Wilberforce was visibly perturbed. "What are you going to do then?"

"I'm going to light a fire, then I'm going to sleep."

"Oh," said Wilber, then after ferreting in the back of the Rover for a couple of minutes he said to Mike, "You'll want this then." and handed him the magnifying glass.

"What am I going to do with this?" Asked Mike.

"Light another fire of course."

"But I can't. It's night time."

"Of course it is. If it wasn't you wouldn't need to light a fire."

"But," said Mike, by way of explanation, "This won't work at night. It only works in the sunshine."

"What sort of a stupid sorcerer are you? What's the use of a spell that won't light fires at night?"

"Well you didn't say it had to work at night. You asked me to light a fire in the day."

"But any fool knows," said Wilber, his exasperation overcoming his timidity, "That you don't need to start fires in the middle of the day. You need fires at night."

"Well I didn't know what you meant." Mike snarled. "Anyway, it doesn't work and I'll have to find another way to do it."

After searching around in the Rover Mike managed to find two long pieces of wire which he attached to the battery. Then he gathered some wood by the light of the headlights and soaked it in petrol from one of the Jerry cans. Then, placing the wood on the ground he stroked the two wires together beside the wood and a shower of sparks immediately set the petrol soaked wood alight. Wilberforce stood to one side, a study in stark terror.

"You may be loony," he said to nobody in particular, "But you sure are powerful." He could no longer decide which was the more frightening, Miko or the woods.

Once Mike had built the fire up to a reasonable size and gathered what he thought would be enough wood to see him through the darkness, he climbed, fully clothed, into his sleeping bag and lay down. He was just relaxing when Wilberforce said

"Miko, What are you doing now?"

"I'm going to sleep. What do you think I'm doing?"

"But what about the Banshee? He'll drive you mad and take your soul."

"You'll drive me mad if you don't shut up and let me get some rest."

There was a short pause and then;

"Miko, do you mind if I go back to the school now? I promise to comeback in the morning."

Mike sat up and tried to speak calmly through his clenched teeth.

"I don't care if you go into the jaws of death itself as long as you let me get some peace." He turned over, threw a log on the fire and sent up a great shower of sparks. By the time he had laid down again Wilberforce had disappeared. .

By his own estimate Mike slept about two hours before he was woken up. This time it was by strange noises in the wood and even stranger feelings in his head. The world was tilting in all directions and Mike felt as though he had woken up in a drunken stupor. His annoyance at being woken up overcame all feelings of surprise or fear. He shouted, cursed and threatened the agency that wakened him and, after a five-minute tirade of abuse he noticed that the ground was, once again, standing still. He snuggled back down into the sleeping bag when a voice said,

"That's not fair. You're supposed to be afraid of me, not to threaten me and stand up to me."

"Who the devil are you? If you'll just show yourself I'll murder you quickly and get some sleep."

"Why can't we talk about this? Look, you're the first person I've seen in years who doesn't run a mile at the thought of me."

"We can't talk about it because I'm tired, exhausted and ready to drop."

"You're already lying down so you can't be ready to drop. - I don't know though, being prone doesn't prevent you from being ready to drop if your existing support were removed. The important word in that construction is ready. What do you think?"

"I think I am going totally bananas. Where are you? Come out into the light so that I can see you."

"You'll have to promise not to get violent."

"I promise I promise. Cross my heart and hope to die," Mike screamed, searching his childhood memory for any other oaths which might carry weight in this crazy place.

"Okay, here I come."

Mike looked carefully and at the edge of the firelight a shape appeared.

At first it looked like a patch of fog but after a while it firmed up and turned into a white sheet draped over a large pumpkin standing atop a long pole. At least, that's how it looked to Mike.

"Are you some sort of ghost?" he asked.

"Most certainly not," replied the shape. "I'm a card carrying banshee. There aren't many of us left these days."

I'm not surprised if you go around waking people up pointlessly in the night."

"That's not fair. I only wanted some conversation. I don't often get the chance of talking to other people. Particularly sorcerers. Normally people are afraid of me and they usually die of fright when I come to talk with them."

"I'm not surprised after that trick you did with the earth and the sky. When I came to I didn't know which way was up."

"Oh that wasn't real. I did that with your mind. I'm very big with minds. Most of us banshees are you know. By the way, my name's O'Banion and you're Miko the sorcerer. How's that for an introduction."

"Rotten. You're supposed to let me tell you my own name, How'd you know anyway?"

"I picked it up from Wilberforce's mind. He thinks you're the most powerful loony in the world. He's not a gremlin you know. He's a goblin but he's too forgetful, like most of his kind. They'd forget their names if they weren't tattooed on at birth. The only thing they can ever remember properly is their way home. After all, you never heard of a goblin getting lost, did you?" Mike had to admit, once again, that he never had.

Now that O'Banion had Mike in his clutches he seemed determined to continue talking for as long as possible but as the time passed Mike found himself becoming more and more interested in the things the banshee had to say.

"Of course, you know why they've brought you here don't you. They're fighting the trolls again. It happens every so often. The problem is this time there are no young people left. They've all gone off to the cities. Why work at the old crafts when you can make a fortune on a production line for General Brooms. Then of course there's the effect of specialised education, hundreds of people who can levitate and nobody who can catch a unicorn. And they have no respect for their elders. I've been around for some three thousand years but you'd think I arrived yesterday the way they treat me.

"I'm not surprised if you keep frightening them all the time."

"Alright. I'm sorry about that. But it's still true that you have a problem on your hands with the trolls. A cousin of mine has a place down in the south and he's had no end of trouble with them. You know, like setting fire to his trees and painting their names on the ground."

"Why doesn't he 'take their souls' as Wilberforce calls it."

"Ah well. There you have a problem with trolls again. They're very limited in their perception. Most of them would never notice that it was gone. You might even say they're as thick as their own stone blocks. You know, dead stupid. They have to be to keep attacking the rest of the world. That's only my opinion mind you."

"I thought you said they might win this time."

"They might, but that doesn't make it sensible does it? Just think of history. When the dwarves lost the 'War of the Runes' with the wizards it didn't do them any harm did it? The wizards were broke for years after despite winning, weren't they?"

"I don't really know," said Mike

"Well it doesn't, it didn't and they were respectively," said O'Banion snappily. You haven't done much background work on this have you?"

"Well I couldn't really. I was only offered the job this afternoon and there seems to be a shortage of general work for sorcerers if they don't want to work for Axel and company."

"That's true, said O'Banion thoughtfully, "But if I were you I'd ask for a written contract. Once the war's over they're sure to try and weasel out of the deal."

"That's twice you've mentioned this war they're fighting. How does that affect my deal with Axel?"

"You are their secret weapon."

"What?" screamed Mike. "I'll say it's secret. I don't know a thing about it."

"Haven't you got a job description or anything? I'm beginning to think Wilberforce is right. You are a loony sorcerer."

"Its all every well for you," Mike shouted, "You know your way around this place but I just found myself sitting beside a tree with a group of gibbering idiots offering me a job. Now what have I gotten myself into?"

Seeing Mike's outrage O'Banion decided that it would be best to calm his companion down, Speaking softly and using his considerable powers of persuasion he explained the background to the troll's invasion and the shortage of manpower. He also explained that that Mike was the last hope of the guilds for finding a lasting solution to the problem. Preferably by wiping the trolls out. After the explanation was finished Mike sat and thought awhile.

"Okay," he said eventually, "Let me see if I've got this straight. The trolls come out of the south every hundred years or so and attack the rest of the world, or at least this continent. In the past they've always been beaten but this year it looks as though they might have the muscle to do it."

"That's about the bones of the situation."

"What happens if I refuse to help?"

"Axel will probably send you home and pay your expenses."

"No. I mean what happens to the dwarves, the faeries, the elves and all the other unlikely folk I've met in this place?"

"They will all fight, and they may even win. But in another hundred years the trolls will try again and there will be fewer young people to fight. They're sure to win eventually.

"And then what happens?"

"Nobody knows. They've never won before so there's nothing to go on but supposition. But why worry? As a sorcerer you can fix them up in no time."

"But I'm not a sorcerer, I'm an engineer."

"Yes, I know all about that. You're all the same. You all swear blind that you're not sorcerers but you all come across with the goods in the end. You just like to be secretive, that's all."

"Wait a minute, what do you mean 'We all'? Have you dealt with sorcerers before?"

"Well, not me personally, like I said, most people run away from me, but I've seen sorcerers hired by other people and they always act the same way that you do. They always pretend to know nothing of magic."

"But I don't know any magic," said Mike feeling quite dejected.

"That's what they all say." said O'Banion "But they manage to devise some marvelous spells. Mind you, not many of them are loony enough to get themselves involved in a war they know nothing about. The others just sorted out farming problems or found spells to improve the quality of love potions or summer wine."

"I'm beginning to agree with Bandor and Wilberforce," Mike thought, "I am loony."

"You shouldn't think things like that, even if they are true. Anyway, the fact that you do think them means they're not. If you were a loony you wouldn't think you were. You'd think you weren't. Therefore anyone who thinks he is; is not. Whereas thinking you are not does not mean that you are because if you think you're not, you might be or you might not be, whereas if you think you are you're probably not. That's a rather good point for philosophical discussion don't you think?"

"I don't know. I just think it's rude to listen to other people's thoughts when they're not thinking to you."

"Well you shouldn't think so loudly."

"I can't help it. I'm agitated."

"Yes Miko, I can see that. If you lie down I'll put you back to sleep until Wilberforce gets back."

Mike lay down in his sleeping bag and closed his eyes. It occurred to him to ask the banshee how he would induce this sleep but before he could do so he had slipped into unconsciousness. O'Banion slowly faded into a patch of mist that floated over to where Mike lay on the floor of the woods

"You are," he thought, "A very powerful sorcerer. I can see that much in your mind. You're also quite loony, but you didn't run out of my forest and you stayed up half the night talking to me when you could have been nasty and beastly. I shall, for what it may be worth, give you any help that I can." The mist flowed over Mike's body and disappeared without any change. Thus it was that Miko the Sorcerer received the invisible protection of a banshee.

The School

In the morning Mike was wakened by Wilberforce shouting and pulling his arm.

"Come on Miko, we have to leave quickly." The little goblin was highly agitated and spent most of his time looking over his shoulder. So much time did he spend looking behind him that Mike was convinced that anybody could have approached from the front without being seen,

"Stop worrying Wilber, nobody's going to come out of the woods and attack us," Mike said as he shook himself out of his sleeping bag and put everything into the Rover. Then he checked the petrol and water supply, started the engine and called Wilberforce to get in. The goblin needed no second bidding and sat in silent misery as Mike headed out of the forest.

As little sleep as Mike had had, it was enough and he made much better speed in the half dark that was forest daylight than he had the night before.

After little more than an hour they reached the edge of the woodland and burst out into the spring sunshine.

"Thank goodness for that." said Wilber, looking visibly more relaxed, then he looked around the Land Rover to see if any ghoul or ghost had clung to it for a free ride, There were none so he looked across at Mike and said,

"You must be the most powerful sorcerer ever Miko. How did you survive the night without being attacked or devoured by the banshee?"

"I told them if they touched me I'd set you on to them."

"You didn't. You couldn't have. You didn't mention my name did you?" The goblin's agitation was plain so Mike did not have the heart to say that the banshee already knew Wilber's name before he left the forest,

"No," he laughed, "I didn't mention your name."

Wilber relaxed again and sat in silence for another fifteen minutes until the track they were following came to an abrupt end.

"Where's the road gone?" asked Mike, looking for any sign of a continuation.

"Ah. I thought you might ask that. We seem to have reached a faerie ring."

"Fine, How do we get round it through it or over it?"

"I don't know. You're the sorcerer. It's your equipment."

Mike sat and quietly tried to contain his rising wrath. He resisted the urge to take Wilberforce by the neck and shake him until his teeth fell out. "Look Wilberforce, I'm just a poor demented sorcerer. I wouldn't know a faerie ring if I heard it. I have no idea how small or large it is or what I may, or may not, say or do, on it, in it, or to it. If there is a penalty I don't know what that penalty might be. Now either you explain it to me slowly and clearly or I just drive straight ahead and we take our chances."

"NO!" screamed Wilberforce, Don't do that. If you go into a faerie ring you never come out. At least, nobody ever has yet. If you can't find a way of getting over it without making contact with it we'll just have to go back the way we came and make a three day detour,"

"Why can't we ask the faeries to let us across?"

"The faeries? Let us across? For nothing? You must be joking. That tight fisted bunch would sell their grannies for a pinch of stardust. Especially when they have you over a barrel."

"Well you're mixing you metaphors but I think I understand what you mean, What about that girl Lutetia ? Can't she do something for us ?"

"I doubt it but I can get her out here if you like. Just don't move this equipment of yours whatever you do." In a twinkle Wilberforce was gone and Mike sat alone. Then, in another twinkle the seat beside him was occupied by Lutetia.

"What is the problem then?" she asked, with a very superior pout on her face.

"This lack of road in front of us is a faerie ring," said Mike, calmly. "We need it moved if I'm ever going to get to the school."

"My life, is that all," Lutetia exploded. "You just need faerie ring moved. Never mind that it took a great deal of time to construct, that doesn't matter. Never mind that a lot of people invested a lot of their time and money in selecting this location, that's not important. Never mind that moving it will cost a fortune and ruin a lot of its properties, not to mention upsetting local house prices. None of that matters because Miko the sorcerer has to get to the school. Well let me tell you mister Miko.... That ring stays where it is unless you're prepared to foot the bill for moving plus dislocation allowance, plus loss of profits, er.. plus a two percent negotiating fee for me, plus.."

"Hold it." Mike shouted. Lutetia immediately stopped and started to cringe in the passenger seat. "You are right. It would be too inconvenient all round. I'll just go home and leave it to the trolls and their dragons. I gather from Wilberforce that they won't be able to get out if they happen to get in."

Lutetia's face turned a cloudy purple colour.

"Let's not be hasty about this," she said as Mike turned the Rover around, "maybe I can get you a discount. As a friend of the family."

Mike stopped the Rover but left the engine running.

"If it's anything less than one hundred percent, forget it. I want that ring out of the way in fifteen minutes or I'm going home."

"Well! Some people." said Lutetia and disappeared. She was back again in ten minutes.

"They're moving it, but it sure didn't earn you any friends."

"I'm surprised they are bothering if they are all as hard nosed as you."

"Well I did tell them that you were very powerful."

"That doesn't seem to cut much ice around here. What sort of powerful?"

"Well I told them that your brother-in-law was on the Urban Planning Authority and your father was in the Building Department of the Westown administration."

Mike was about to explode with anger when, instead he burst out laughing.

"Its no joke," cried Lutetia. "When they find out that you don't have any pull in this place they are going to be mad. It was only the promise of favours to come that persuaded them to do it."

"Oh well, as long as they do it," said Mike, "I don't care who they think my family are," and he turned the Rover back to face the ring, only to find that it wasn't there.

"Well, so much for all the hard work and expense of moving it," he said as he moved the Land Rover forward. But nobody heard him because Lutetia had disappeared. The rest of the journey was uneventful. Mike followed the flat, unmetalled surface of the track for another two hours and found himself approaching a walled city. As he arrived at the wall he drove into an opening which professed to be the 'Four O'Clock' gate.

He had been without company for much of the time because the only person who sat with him was Wilberforce, and he only did so occasionally to check the route Mike was following. As the Rover drove through the gate Axel suddenly appeared in passenger seat.

"Ah, Miko," he said, with a friendly smile, "I'm so glad you've arrived. You'd better let me navigate or you'll be bombarded with questions." Axel gave precise, detailed instructions on the basis that sorcerers should be treated like children and Mike followed them to the letter. He eventually pulled the Land Rover into a narrow alley that opened onto a cobbled quadrangle. Two complete sides of the quadrangle were in the form of cloistered arches and third side that he could see appeared to be filled with antique shops with no glass in the windows

When he had stopped the engine and climbed out of the Rover Mike examined the fourth side which contained the entrance arch. It was a pub, or maybe a restaurant looking rather like some of the things Mike had seen in the older cities of Europe. There were tables outside and people were sitting around drinking and eating oblivious of the fact that it was eleven in the morning.

"Just what I need," said Mike, "A long cold beer." Axel led Mike over to a table surrounded by the other members of Axel's committee and filled with tankards of ale.

"We looked it up in Axel's book, Miko," said Esmeralda. "It says that sorcerers always consume great quantities of ale while they work."

Mike lifted one of the tankards which was untouched and raised it to his lips. At the first sip he knew he had made a mistake. He spat the liquid out, all over Bandor, and began searching for something to extinguish the fire in his head.

Bandor wiped himself down with a cloth and spluttered, "Not just a loony, but a softy as well. He can't even drink a man's drink."

Mike continued drinking the glass of water that somebody had brought him and did not appear to hear what Bandor had said.

"I'll bet he prefers those soft elven drinks," continued the dwarf. "Some sorcerer we've hired ourselves. He's probably afraid of his own shadow." The confidence of Bandor's diatribe was increasing as Mike failed to react.

"I'll bet any of the dwarf children could tie him in knots with no effort. We've wasted our money. I suggest we pay him off now and send a small group of highly paid dwarves to sort out the trolls."

As Bandor continued Mike finished the water and walked over to the Rover. He rummaged in a box in the back and soon came up with what he wanted. It was a roll of exceedingly sticky waterproof adhesive tape.

He took it back and placed it on the table. Bandor was still in full flood. Mike asked Leander which was the ale the elves preferred, picked up a tankard of it and stepped over to Bandor. Before Bandor knew what was happening Mike had poured the tankard's contents over the dwarf's head. Bandor's reaction was swift and sure. He stepped back from Mike and in one fluid motion pulled the axe from his belt and raised it over his head to bifurcate anybody who came close enough.

Mike had been expecting this and stepped forward when Bandor stepped back.

As the dwarf raised the axe above his head Mike used his height to grasp the top of the shaft and forcibly release it from Bandor's grip. He threw the axe carelessly over his shoulder and then applied an arm lock to his struggling opponent. With Bandor held fuming and shouting, Mike picked up the roll of adhesive tape with his free hand and taped Bandor's mouth firmly shut. The result, among other things, was complete silence. He then heaved the struggling dwarf into one of the empty seats and taped him firmly to it.

"Now perhaps we can have a little peace and quiet," he said as he examined the rest of the tankards on the table. "We sorcerers take our drinking very seriously and I don't want it spoiled by the petty grievances of silly little dwarves."

The faces of the surrounding group had gone through a series of transformations during the brief activity. Some of them had been impressed with the way Bandor had stood up to the sorcerer. Now they were doubly impressed by the fearlessness of Miko's reactions and the power of his spells.

"Er.. Miko," Axel said, as he nervously produced book after book from under his cloak and laid them on the table. "That's a very powerful spell you've put on Bandor. Um.. How long will it last?

"It will last until somebody takes it off again. I'm not going to do it, but you may if you wish. The only thing I will say is that if the person concerned ever speaks to, or about, me like that again, I shall have to put a more permanent stop an his tongue."

"Yes. Yes. But does that mean that anybody can take that spell off of Bandor?"

"Sure, but there are ways and ways of removing that spell."

"Good. Good. But does that mean that anybody could have put it on."

"Yes, anybody who could overcome Bandor could put it on,"

Axel and Esmeralda were looking closely at the bindings while Bandor fumed in them. Leander, leading the rest of the group, pointedly ignored the whole issue and acted as though the dwarf was sitting normally. While Axel and Esmeralda discussed the technical merits of the spell that Mike had cast over Bandor the others fell into desultory conversation about the quality of ale. Mike, meanwhile, had found a brew he really liked. It was more like liquid sunshine than liquid fire. He was prevented from learning any more about the ale by a tap on the shoulder. He turned to find himself facing a man so like Irving that he could only be another gnome. This one, however, did not carry a fishing rod.

"Excuse me," he said, somewhat shakily, "but if you aren't going to kill our companion could you release him so that we can finish our game?"

Mike looked to where the gnome was pointing and saw another dwarf fixed with his axe above his head. He had been prevented from throwing it by the arrival of Bandor's axe which had passed through the cloth of his sleeve and pinned him firmly to the wall. Mike took first the axe from the dwarf's hand, then the other from his sleeve and put them both in his own belt. Then he spoke in his most majestic voice.

"Never draw weapons on a sorcerer for he who hesitates before he leaps gathers no moss, so it is written."

The dwarf's companions looked at Mike in silent awe and the dwarf himself sat down looking pale and shaken. Mike returned to his companions. When he sat down again at the table Mike noticed that Bandor was missing. Leander explained that Axel had taken him off as a research project for a couple of advanced Kinetics students. Mike decided that, as Axel was the only one worth asking about the troll situation, he would spend all his available time finding out more about his surroundings.

The quadrangle in which he stood turned out to be the recreation area used by the school staff and the senior research students. The open fronted antique shops were full of what everybody called scientific apparatus, although Mike did not recognise any of it. Mike was asked to move the Rover to a particular corner of the yard which contained, among other things, a number of brooms. When he showed some curiosity about these it was explained that the service staff and suchlike could not teleport themselves so they used the next best means of transport, the broom. Mike had parked in the broom park.

Wilberforce showed Mike to a room which would be his for his entire stay at the school. Axel had an apartment across the hall and Esmeralda lived about three minutes walk away. Mike stowed his gear in the room and washed himself in cold water. This done he decided to go back to the bar and await Axel's return.

As Mike stepped out of the room he bumped into the man he intended to wait for. Axel had a big smile on his face and it blossomed even larger when he saw Mike.

"Miko, Miko, you're just the chap I've been looking for. That spell you cast on Bandor was remarkable. My students eventually came up with a way of overcoming it but it wasn't easy. Now they are working on a method of simulating it cheaply so that anybody can cast it. You really are going to be worth your money when it comes to fighting the trolls."

"Oh yes, the trolls. I'd like to discuss that with you."

"Yes. Yes. I know, but first Bandor has something he would like to say to you. Come this way please." Axel walked off leaving Mike to follow. The tall wizard was still talking when Mike caught him at the bar.

"What was that about Bandor.. ?"

"Ah yes. Bandor wants to tell you...Here he is now. He can tell you himself."

Bandor approached firmly and resolutely from the side of the bar. In his hands he carried two flagons of the elven ale that Mike had found so palatable.

"Miko," he said looking upward into Mike's eyes, "I said some very foolish things earlier on. I know I was full of the winter ale but that was no excuse. From now on I shall swear off the winter ale and drink only this elven summer wine. If you can drink this and be man enough to disarm a drunken dwarf then I can be dwarf enough to fight the trolls along side you. Please join me in a drink.

There was an embarrassed silence as Mike weighed up Bandor's words. Then he took one of the flagons from the dwarf's hands and raised it.

"I will drink with you Bandor and I suggest that everybody here drinks to you. To Bandor. I give you a toast in the ancient tongue of the sorcerers 'Tee equals two pie rootel upon gee'." Mike emptied his flagon and everybody in the bar began shouting and drinking and trying to repeat the toast. The other dwarf whom Mike had disarmed earlier also swore to drink only summer wine and then proceeded to get monumentally drunk on it just to demonstrate the manliness of the brew.

Axel drew Mike to one side.

"We can't talk here, it's too noisy. And we can't do any real planning until we have the whole of the negotiating committee together and sober. That probably won't happen for a week. I suggest that yourself and Bandor come along to my apartment for dinner tonight. I'll get Esmeralda along and, provided that my wife doesn't do too much damage to your stomach with her cooking, we can talk about the war."

Mike very much wanted to talk about the war but thought Axel was probably right. He had noticed earlier that Leander and Wilberforce were drinking themselves under the table and, whilst they would make excellent company, they would not help a lot with information. Irving was shaking his fishing rod at a group of gnomes and looked set for a long discussion, Lutetia had not been seen since the faerie ring incident and Esmeralda had taken Pallisy home because the excitement proved too much for her. Mike agreed to leave further discussion until dinner and said that he would walk around the town until then, just to get the feel of the place.

He had two hours to kill and decided that if he walked about three blocks in each direction from the quadrangle he would get a good idea of the character of the town and have enough time to wash up before dinner,

It was impossible to walk in blocks but Mike managed to navigate himself around. He started off approximately sunward and walked for about a mile, then he crossed the street and walked back the other way, occasionally making small detours to the side. When he arrived back at the school entrance he turned through ninety degrees and repeated the process. On the first two excursions he had walked along wide, well paved streets. On the third he found himself in a small winding lane which kept breaking off into numerous smaller winding lanes.

He had to concentrate hard to ensure that he did not get lost. So hard, in fact, that he did not see his assailants until they were upon him.

There were three of them and they came out of a side alley. The first grabbed him around the neck from behind and tried to pull him down while the other two tried to punch large holes in his body. They were unlucky. Mike's natural build and his work in Canada had combined to make him a hard man to damage. Nonetheless his attackers tried.

Using the man holding his neck as a support Mike brought both his feet up from the floor and kicked out savagely at chest height catching one man full in the chest and raking the edge of his boot down the side of the other's forward bent head.

As his feet fell back to the ground he prepared to pull forward and when he did so the man behind was caught by his own attempts to keep from stumbling under Mike's weight. Mike bent forward as hard as he could, ignoring the pain from the grip on his neck, and the man behind was pulled upward and forward off of his feet. Mike bent so low that his attacker went over his head and was forced to release his grip. Mike stood up again to get a sight of the three men. One lay on the floor and two stood facing him. This improved the odds very slightly and Mike, eager to take advantage of any factor in his favour, jumped forward and landed on the chest of the man lying down. Using it as a springboard he jumped off to the right and cannoned into the groggier looking of the remaining two who went down like a skittle.

The remaining one caught Mike's arm as he rebounded and tried to tear it off and hit him with it. Instead of resisting Mike went forward with the pull and drove his knee into his opponent's midriff. The man doubled up and Mike gave him a Hammer blow behind the ear with the side of his fist.

All three of his opponents were down but not out. Mike knew that if it came to a long fight three fit men would beat one fit man, and if nothing else these three were fit. He appraised them very quickly. They were medium height, thickly muscled with broad necks and deep chests. They seemed to have been struck from the same mould.

The appraisal convinced Mike that now was a good time to be somewhere else and he wished he knew Axel's trick of teleportation. Not knowing it he did the next best thing.

He ran as fast as he could back in the direction he had come from, His attackers quickly regained their feet but did not seem keen to chase him. He was thankful for this and was both glad and breathless when he reached the school again.

The Briefing

Once back in his room Mike examined the damage he had picked up in the fight. His fists were bruised at the knuckles and his neck was red and swollen. He had a black eye and a chest that would probably end up looking like a chequer board. He also thought they had cracked a couple of his ribs. He washed himself to clear his head and the blood from his body. He gained a little satisfaction from knowing that at least some of it belonged to the others.

After tidying himself as best he could he put on a clean shirt and crossed the hall to Axel's front door. Mike's descriptions were enough to convince Axel that the attackers were trolls come into the city to sound out the opposition. They were enough to convince Axel's wife Morag that all sorcerers were mad. She did, however, take the time and trouble to bind Mike's chest and provide a remarkable treatment for his black eye which returned it to normal appearance in minutes. Mike surveyed himself after the treatment and the improvement in his appearance was enough to make him feel like eating. At the mention of food Morag flew into the kitchen and there followed some of the best cursing that Mike had ever heard. When Morag came back it was obvious that diner would be, at the very least delayed.

"Do not worry my dear," said Axel "You were right in the first place, I should have arranged dinner. Just wait a moment please." He disappeared from the room and returned a few minutes later with yet another large leather bound book. After a few moments of mumbling he suddenly said "Yes. That should do the trick. We can start when the others arrive."

When all the guests had arrived they sat down around an empty table. Axel performed a few passes with his hands and suddenly the table was loaded with such food as Mike had not seen in ages. For the next five minutes all the talk was of the economics of bringing in food rather than cooking it oneself, Nobody mentioned Morag's debacle in the kitchen.

After eating too much and taking too much wine the talk turned again to the war with the trolls and the attack which had been made on Mike earlier. It was the opportunity Mike had been waiting for.

"It seems to me that I have accepted a very bad bargain," he said. "I gather from various sources that you expect me to help fight the trolls. I don't know anything about trolls, or fighting for that matter, so I'm not sure that I can deliver what you want. I'm also particularly cowardly and averse to pain."

This brought a general hubbub of comments from all of the company. When it had died down it was Esmeralda who spoke.

"I did some further checking this afternoon and it seems that this is another standard ploy used by sorcerers when they first arrive." She produced some scribbled notes and began to read aloud. "Sorcerers are usually particularly creative at such activities as warfare, building, town planning and the solution of unusual problems. They are not good at housework, shopping, negotiating or following orders. In many cases their responsibilities have to be spelled out to them before they will co-operate and frequently they require cajoling, threatening or exposure to personal danger before they will produce their best work." She folded the piece of paper and placed it in the small green velvet bag she carried.

"That," she continued, "came from no less an authority than Bendingale's History of Sorcery."

"Well it seems to match the comments Axel made earlier yesterday when Miko arrived," said Bandor. "The problem seems to be 'how do we motivate Miko to fulfill his part of the deal. Threats wouldn't work, appeals to his better nature might have some impact, and that only leaves...'"

"Wait a minute," Interrupted Mike, "I am not a sack of potatoes to be bargained over. I make my own decisions. Tell me something about the trolls."

"What do you want to know Miko '?"

"Well for instance, what do they look like ?"

"You saw some today. They attacked you." "I Know. But they just looked like thickset men. Trolls are supposed to have long fangs, carry clubs and eat babies and things like that."

"I don't know where you get this stuff from Miko," Esmeralda answered, "but whoever teaches you needs straightening out. It's always the same with sorcerers. You have a lousy social education. Trolls do not eat babies any more than anybody else does. They look like short, thickset men because that's what they are. They don't carry clubs, or dress in dragon skins or live in caves or turn to stone when they die.

They do fight ferociously, they are disgustingly fit and healthy and they keep very much to themselves when they are not fighting with the Midlands. We don't know much about their culture because we spend most of our time fighting them."

"And damned fine fighting men they are." added Bandor. "Why, I remember back in the battle of ...

"Okay Bandor," said Axel. "I think Miko gets the message."

"Why are they at war with you?" asked Mike.

The silence that followed deafened everybody.

"Could you er.. explain the question please Miko?" asked Axel.

"Well, you know, what do they want, why do you have to fight them? What do you have that they are after?"

"I'm sorry Miko, I still don't understand"

Mike began to get exasperated.

"Well if you are fighting a war you have to be fighting over something. You have to have a reason. An aggressor and an aggresee. Otherwise the war doesn't work and you all go home again. In this case I assume that the trolls count as the aggressor and want something that you do not wish them to have. So what is it?"

"Miko you are raising some very interesting philosophical points which I'm sure we could discuss profitably with a sorcerer at any other time but at the moment there is a war on and I don't quite see where your ideas can profitably lead us." Axel looked perplexed as he spoke.

"Just a minute Miko," said Bandor, perhaps we can straighten this out by outlining the ground rules for war. The trolls live in Southend which is... Axel, do you have a map?

Axel tapped the top of the table and it suddenly became a map.

"Thank you. Now Miko, the trolls live down here in Southend. Their main city is Monolith, which contains about half a million of them, and there are probably as many again living in the small hamlets around and about the place.

Now, we are cut off from them by two major geographical features, these are the sneaky peaks and the dragon swamps. It is practically impossible to reach Midland by any other means than the troll gate. Are you with us so far?"

Mike nodded, as did Axel, Morag and Esmeralda.

"Now the trolls have suddenly started moving out of the troll gate and they may be bringing dragons with them."

"And?" asked Mike.

"And what?"

"And why are you fighting them?"

"But I just explained all that."

"Yes, he just explained all that."

"No he didn't. All he said was the trolls are coming out through the troll gate."

"YES".

"Yes WHAT ??? Are you saying that the only reason for fighting the trolls is that they are coming out of their own country? Or have they been attacking people?"

"There's no chance of that. As soon as it started we sent an expeditionary force to deal with them. After all, we couldn't let them get away with that"

"With what?"

"Whatever they would have done if we had let them."

"What would they have done?"

"Nothing. We stopped them didn't we?"

"Wait a minute. Wait a minute. You sent an expeditionary force."

"Yes ,"

"What happened then?"

"They were massacred."

"Who?"

"The expeditionary force."

"And then what happened?"

"As soon as the people heard about the massacre they were incensed. They wanted revenge on the trolls for the outrage they had committed. That's why the guilds had a whip round and decided to hire a sorcerer."

"And that's me."

"Yes. That's you. Now do you understand?"

"No," said Mike, "And I don't think I ever shall. Let's go through it just once more from the beginning."

Monolith

If ever a place was misnamed it was Monolith. The architecture was diverse and interesting and the variety of materials used added to the general impression of a well designed, well managed city. The major building in the city was a granite construction which rose some sixty yards into the air and dominated all the surrounding development. This was the building which had given the city its name.

As the seat of government it housed, among other things, the Southend Planning Authority. Overseeing this authority was Bellman. He sat listening intently to a group of three people.

"We found him easily," said the first

"He didn't try to hide," added the second.

"Unusually confident, he was," put in the third.

"Alright, alright," snapped Bellman, fighting to recover his temper, "Let me make sure I understand this. You went into the city of Westown and kept watch on the school. A strange looking man arrived, on an even stranger looking transport, which certainly wasn't based on brooms, and you assumed he was the sorcerer they had hired.

"Yes."

"That's right."

"Unusually big he was."

"Okay, just suppose the guilds have hired a sorcerer, what do they hope to gain by it. There isn't a sorcerer born who could stand up to us."

"That's true chief."

"Yes, that's true."

"Unusually tough he was."

"But even assuming all this to be true, what in the name of the gods did you hope to accomplish by bringing him here. Everyone knows that sorcerers will only work for the guilds and that they eat babies. Can you imagine the havoc it would have caused if you had brought him here and he had managed to get loose. The people are jittery enough as it is.

Only this week we had a great petition in from the landsmen asking to delay the journey for another five years. it's a hundred years since we tried last time but the people have longer memories these days and are very jittery. If we brought in a captive sorcerer we would have riots in the streets."

"Sorry Bellman."

"We just thought you would want to see him."

"Unusually good fighter he was."

"Alright. I believe you may be right. About him being a sorcerer that is, so don't say anything to anybody until I've had a chance to discuss it with the council. In the meantime you had better get something to eat and have those wounds cleaned up. He must have been one remarkable sorcerer to do that to the three of you."

"He was Bellman."

"Sure enough Bellman"

"Unusually fast he was."

When the three had left Bellman, leader of the Clan of Bellmen and senior councilman of the Southend Planning Authority, sat and considered the information his agents had given him. He would have to be very careful at the council meeting if he wanted to remain in control. He took five more minutes deciding on his strategy for the meeting and then left to prepare himself.

The council chamber was full when Bellman arrived for the meeting. He walked from the back of the room to the front and took his position at the centre of the large horseshoe table at which the councilmen sat. The council was composed of the senior man from each of the clans that occupied a place in Southend life. The layout was simple. As head of the largest clan Belman was senior councilman and sat in the middle of the table. Next to him sat the next most powerful and so on down to the smallest clan. Next to Bellman sat Landsman and Roadman and farthest from him sat Barman and Fireman. Each occupied his position by heredity and each was considered to be a shining example of Troll gentry.

Bellman banged his gavel down.

"Gentlemen, we are in session. May I take it that we have read and approved the minutes of the last meeting?" There was no argument and the minutes were accepted. "Now," continued Bellman, "Last time we were together I asked you to think about who should lead the march out of Southend and consequently take the brunt of the guilds attack. Who wishes to comment?"

Several hands were raised. Bellman recognised that of Dustman.

"I think we all know the feelings of my clan by now. We have led the march on three past occasions and we have felt proud to do so. This time we would feel proud again, but, and this is a very big but, we don't have the trollpower to do it. One hundred years ago we lost eighty out of every hundred and we have not made up for it yet. We would not mind if this was typical but it isn't. Salesman can tell you that his clan lost only one in fifty, the landsmen almost did not get into the field and many of you suffered no losses at all. Well this time it's going to be different. My members tell me that they feel put upon. That they are doing all the dirty work while the administrators stay home and get fat looking after supplies and doing no fighting. They feel that, as a working class clan, they are being used. That is why we are insistent that we make use of the dragon that has come our way by good fortune." Dustman began to warm to his subject as Bellman had hoped. The other councillors were beginning to either nod in agreement or shake their heads in disagreement. Within five minutes the meeting was in uproar.

"Gentlemen, Gentlemen," shouted Bellman, "Please. This is a council meeting, not a ballgame." The room slowly returned to order, "Gentlemen. I feel that some of you may be missing the point. If Dustman's clan is both resentful and depleted then it would be disastrous to let them lead. On the other hand they have a glorious history of leading and I think we should certainly solicit Dustman's advice on how the leader should deploy his forces. But I also think the time has come far a break with the tradition of single clan leadership." He paused to let the hubbub caused by his last remark die down.

"We are not facing the traditional situation of the past. This time the guilds have forced us into a new posture. They have hired a sorcerer."

Bellman might have thrown a live griffin onto the table and not had as much reaction. Everybody present started shouting at once and very little of any consequence was said, Landsman eventually managed to get the floor by shouting louder than anybody else and keeping it up for longer.

"Wait a minute." He bellowed. "Just wait a minute. This puts things in a very different light. We all know that sorcerers have long fangs and eat babies. We all know that they are inhuman monsters who delight in causing pain and misery to all who come in contact with them. We also know that the guilds are just about ruthless enough to employ one. In the face of this break with tradition I would be prepared to listen to any suggestions which would help protect us from the ravages of war with beasts like this. And, I might add, this includes using the dragon as Dustman suggested"

As Landsman finished Bellman knew he had won his battle. The Clans would listen with open ears rather than relying on tradition which said that they should start the journey under the same conditions every time. Now, for the first time in history, they might have a chance to complete the journey.

The Preparation

Mike sat at a large circular table. Alongside him sat Axel and Bandor with the rest of the negotiating committee dispersed further around the table. The whole group looked glum.

"Mike," said Esmeralda, smoothing out her fishnet tights as she spoke, "Are you really telling us that after all our efforts of the past week you still do not understand why we are fighting the trolls,"

"Of course I understand. But I very much doubt if you do. Every time the trolls show their communal face outside Southend, you tear them to pieces. If you don't, then they attack you unmercifully. It seems to me that there is just no good reason for it."

"How can you say that where trolls are concerned?" asked Bandor. "But then, I suppose you've never seen what they can do."

"Oh I'm sure they can be as aggressive as you, and from my own experience they seem to be tough enough. But there must be an underlying reason for it."

"It's obvious," put in Lutetia, glancing up from her copy of the Westown Property Review. "Wherever trolls go the property values fall, the schools get downgraded and the shops fill with those silly wooden clog things that they wear. Trolls are all right in ones but when two or more get together they become objectionable. I certainly wouldn't want them living in my neighborhood."

"You wouldn't want anybody living in your neighborhood." added Irving "Which reminds me. Just the other day two gnomes were refused fishing rights in the river that runs along by your house on the basis that the residents objected. What was all that about?"

Lutetia and Irving drifted off into a private discussion of individual rights and community responsibility. Mike looked round the table again

"Okay," he said, "let's just assume there is a reason for the moment. The question we now face is 'What should we do next?' If Lutetia and Irving will just shut up for a moment Axel can tell us what is likely to happen."

Axel placed a small box about the size of an apple on the table. He began to unfold the sides and continued until the box became a flat surface which filled the table. He passed his hands above the surface and it suddenly became a perfect relief map of the whole country.

"Normally trolls come out of the troll gate and immediately drive straight ahead for Aspic. Sometimes we stop them on the road and sometimes we can't stop them until they begin laying siege to the city. There is even some evidence that they have, in the past, reached as far as attacking Eastham."

Axel stopped to scratch his head under his tall hat. Mike had noticed that he never took it off for any other reason and wondered if he wore it in bed.

"Where does this evidence come from?" interjected Pallisy. "Is it reliable?"

"Well actually it was presented at a conference I attended last year. By Amatheus, you know, that old hermit type who lives over by Millville."

"Really," put in Esmeralda, "I haven't seen him since the night he and I and a couple of others tried to steal a griffin from the Aspic zoo. How is he?

"Oh, he seemed fine. Not as young as he was mind, but in good shape."

Mike banged the table with his boot. "Enough of this. I want information. Data with which I can sorce, as sorcerering seems to be my job. So unless Amatheus is critical information kindly shut up and get on with the story."

"Sorry Miko," several people murmured.

"On a point of order Miko, I'm not sure that it's possible to shut up and get on with the story. Logically and procedurally that is." Mike's cold stare froze Pallisy back into silence.

Axel continued. "The trolls have always favoured the direct approach, not a very subtle people, they move generally northward with the idea of capturing or destroying everything in their path. They take what they can use and they burn what they can't. As I said, not very subtle, but in the long term very expensive on our resources. This time I expect them to use the dragons to get all the speed they can in travelling up from the troll gate and lay siege' to Aspic in about ten days time. That's one thing you can say for the trolls, they are terribly predictable. Once established at Aspic they will come out here and then move on to East Ham."

"In that case we have ten days to build some defenses." said Mike. There was complete silence. It fell on the table like a stone.

"What do you mean Miko, by er.. defences?"

"Well, I mean ways of stopping them overcoming the city. Ways of making them waste their trollpower. Causing maximum losses for any ground they take. Demoralising their forces. All sorts of things."

"But what about attacking them? That's what we always do. We attack them and smash them into the ground."

"In that case you have wasted your money hiring a sorcerer haven't you?"

The silence came back, but this time a little more slowly. Axel broke it.

"Miko, let us get this straight. Are you suggesting that instead of going out to fight the trolls we skulk away in the city while they lay siege to us? Is that what you are suggesting ?"

"In a word, YES ."

"But we never do that." everybody began at once, "We always .. . . .

The detail of what they always.... was lost to Mike in the general hubbub. The argument continued for the next hour but gradually Mike persuaded them that the easiest way to ensure victory over the trolls was to let the trolls knock themselves out laying siege to a well defended, self sufficient city. There was much muttering and disagreement but at least the principle was eventually settled.

"Now," said Axel, "Comes the difficult part."

Mike groaned. Nothing could be more difficult. Could it?

"We have to decide on how the forces are going to be set up. Who gets to command how many of whom?"

Mike listened silently for another hour as the committee argued over the deployment of forces and command. The arguments seemed very familiar. Dwarves did most of the fighting. They would not obey anybody who was not a dwarf. The staff work was done by elves and pixies neither of whom would work for a dwarf. Goblins were only any good as guides and they would work for anybody, probably even the trolls.

As the arguments swung back and forth across the table Mike grew impatient.

"Look," he said finally, unable to contain himself any longer, "as your sorcerer in chief I'll tell you what to do. I'll elect myself commander in chief of the armed forces. Bandor will be the General in charge of fighting, Leander will be the General in charge of planning and Axel will be in charge of communications. You will all need assistants. Bandor can have Irving, Leander can have Pallisy and Axel can have Esmeralda. I want Lutetia and Wilberforce as my personal Aides de Camp."

The response was gratifying. Everybody seemed glad to have the decision made for them but nobody wanted to be seen to allow Mike to get away with anything. They squabbled between themselves for a further five minutes and after that they all accepted Mike's suggestion completely. All he had to do now was instruct them in their individual tasks.

The end of the meeting marked the beginning of a period of intense activity for Mike and the negotiating committee. Having defined their roles Mike found he had to give the committee very specific instructions about their individual duties. He began to learn why they had always just gone out and thumped the trolls as soon as they appeared. The guildsmen could not think of anything else to do. They had no idea whatever of strategy or planning. As Mike laid his plans out before them his reputation as powerful sorcerer grew in leaps and bounds.

Basically Mike's plan was simple. The survival of Westown and the rest of the Midlands depended on being able to wipe out the trolls. According to Axel this meant killing about eighty percent of the troll forces. If this was the case then he would just string the trolls out as thinly as possible so that they were cut off from their home base in the Southlands, and then tear them to pieces. It represented a slight refinement of the usual technique, but only slight.

He had allocated jobs on the basis of the characters of the individuals involved. After the first couple of days his ideas had begun to work out well. Bandor was sent off to round up as many dwarves as he could find who were willing to fight. He was assured that this would be nearly all of the fit males and many of the women. The dwarves were a very aggressive lot. The problem was that they only liked fighting. They did not like training or preparing to fight. Put a group of them together for too long and they would fight each other rather than train to fight somebody else. Bandor's main task was to get the dwarves into groups stationed in the right places so that they could be brought into effect with the minimum effort, This proved to be easy work for him as he was considered something special in terms of ferocity even by the dwarves.

Leander was in charge of planning. Mike had provided him with a large map of the whole country and told him to examine the size of the populations in each of the main towns, and how it would be swelled if the people from the surrounding areas were all brought in. On that basis he would then go on to calculate the amount of food needed to support them all for a week and how much they could store within the security of the city. His lack of aggression and his fear of trolls made him the ideal choice of defence planner.

Axel spent most of his time going from place to place telling various people about the plan and what they could do to aid it. He met with little active enthusiasm but his importance as a wizard was enough to ensure cooperation.

Mike's most important find was in Lutetia and Wilberforce. His own main task, he decided, was to fit out the forces at his command with some sort of adequate weaponry. A quick survey of the dwarfish arms had shown him that the short men were preoccupied with chopping off heads. All of their weapons seemed to be some sort of variant of an axe or a club. If the trolls were to be beaten he had to invent the crossbow quickly. The invention itself was no problem but a supply of suitable raw material for manufacture was a major difficulty. This was where Lutetia and Wilberforce proved to be an amazing team.

Lutetia had contacts everywhere in Midland and always seemed to be able to blackmail or persuade suppliers to give Mike amazing terms for the supply of munitions material. Mike had wondered about this until he accompanied them on the search for arrow or bolt material. Lutetia had first contacted another faerie in Westown and said that she, Mike and Wilber would like to talk about buying wood with particular properties. The three of them went to visit the potential supplier's premises at the appointed time. Once inside, with introductions over, Lutetia began.

"You have the specification of the material we want. What sort of price can you supply at?"

"Well, now, you see that wood is difficult to find, and then we have to bring it on a three day journey to get it to Westown."

"Nonsense," interjected Wilberforce, "You could get it here in less than a day with a good freight broom from the Broomgroves, which is the nearest source of such wood."

"Maybe you could, but freight brooms are too expensive for this type of task."

"No they're not," put in Lutetia. "Give us a price excluding haulage. We can get the stuff here ourselves."

Mike had to cringe as he heard this for earlier in the day he had been told by Lutetia that they were desperately short of brooms for moving equipment. Now she was committing more of the resources they did not have.

"Okay, for the timber cut, bundled and stacked at the cutting site I'll take a pound of gold for every hundred bundles."

Lutetia laughed.

"So would I, but you don't really expect me to pay that price do you? I'll give you two ounces per hundred."

"You want my children to starve? Offering me a price like that? I'd do better selling the stuff as firewood. As a special sacrifice for the war effort - I'll take fourteen ounces"

"My life, everyone should make such sacrifices for the war. Then we'd all be millionaires. Talking of children, yours go to the Westown Faerie academy don't they?"

"Of course, what other school should good faerie children go to?"

"That's right. My uncle is chairman of the board of Governors. If I were to tell him that you are short of money I wonder what effect that would have on your children's chances at school?"

"But I'm not short of money. I make good profits from this business."

"Good. I'm pleased about that, because if you don't agree to supply us at two ounces per hundred bundles I shall have to tell my uncle that you are so poor you cannot afford a contribution to the war effort and that you probably can't manage next years school fees."

"But that's ...

"That's what?"

"That's.. a bargain then. Two ounces of gold per hundred bundles."

"Good," said Lutetia, "We can go now."

"There's just one other thing," said Wilberforce. "I noticed a number of brooms outside which didn't have air tax licenses."

"Oh... er those." squirmed the supplier. "I just happen to have those lying around. I don't use them of course, because they are unlicensed."

"Excellent," smiled Wilber, "In that case you won't mind if we commandeer them for transporting the wood we have just bought."

Chapter seven

After they had left the supplier Mike thought a lot about the tactics he had seen in use. Then he decided not to sit in on any more negotiations.

A Not Too Secret Weapon

The clearing, about the size of four football fields, stood on the top of a steep hill. It was approached by a single track which wound back and forth up the side of the hill and surrounded by a thick fence of wooden stakes that was intended to keep people out rather than in. Within the fence the ground was reasonably level and a mixture of grass and scrubby bushes covered most of the land. As the ground fell away from the summit the hillside was covered in a small forest of tall straight pine trees which had been hacked down in places to provide the track to the top.

Originally there had been a castle on the land but that was centuries ago and all signs of the building had long since disappeared. Now, right in the centre, sat Oriender, the most miserable dragon in the world.

His green and brown scales glinted in the bright sunshine and his long tail was curled round him in a satisfactory way. His powerful back legs were resting feet down and his forelegs were tucked under the base of his neck. His wings, which were streaked with blue, were tucked into his side disguising the length of his back legs and his head rested on the ground with his eyes closed. A slight haze of smoke drifted from his nostrils.

Aleric stood at the entrance to the area. The perimeter fence had a removable portion, which took two men to move it, and made a space large enough to let people in one at a time. He was not afraid of the dragon, but in truth he was not afraid of very much, except possibly his wife (and her mother). He walked towards the giant beast and pondered what he knew of dragons, which was little enough.

This one had landed from exhaustion about a month previously and had just sat there ever since. He knew that mature dragons could only eat in flight and that they usually took their prey on the wing. This one was certainly mature and possibly past it. It was huge and somewhat ungainly on the ground but he knew it would be graceful and lethal in the air.

When Bellman had asked him to take charge of the Dragon he had been to Monolith library to look up the meager records they had on dragon husbandry. He had learned that some very few people had the ability to communicate directly with dragons and indirect communication was all but useless. He, it turned out, could not communicate and had so far been able to make no sense of the dragon's wants or needs.

He had, however, decided that this one would be terrifying if he wanted to be. He did breathe fire and he could crush trolls, or anybody else for that matter, just by walking on them. Perhaps it was just as well that it was content to lie in the field and sleep.

The Trolls who had come to build the fence around the field had been very concerned for the first day or so until they realised that the dragon was relatively docile, at least for the time being.

There was a small trough in the centre of the field, which provided water for the sleeping dragon, and even Aleric had been concerned about filling it the first time, but now it was just another job to be undertaken twice each day.

Bellman had asked for Aleric's assessment of the Dragon as a weapon for the journey and the troll warrior took his responsibility very seriously. He had assessed the size of the beast and its ability to clear ground. Aleric was convinced that the Dragon could walk through almost any building he had ever seen in Midland. The fire breathing would help to spread terror among the Guild folk, but in reality the dragon was not a weapon.

Oriender had slept through most of the time since he had fallen out of the sky above Monolith into this large comfortable field. Now, after several weeks of inactivity, Oriender was beginning to worry slightly. His scales were drying out and he could think of no easy way to get them moistened again. He knew he could not take off again, but equally he knew he needed to fly if he was ever to assuage his hunger. It was a real problem for him.

The troll who came to see him each day seemed nice enough but was not one of the few blessed with ability to communicate, so he had no way of telling the trolls what he needed. He would have to think of something soon or he would start to lose his body weight and, whilst that might help him to get around more easily on land, he would lose the muscles which drove his powerful wings. It was, he had to admit, a problem.

Bellman, Dustman, Landsmen and a few lesser dignitaries had been in to see him but there were none who could communicate with him. He had decided just to doze the time away until he could find someone, anyone, who could speak to him directly. He was confident that something would turn up. And if it didn't he was quite happy to die in peace. It was shame that he wouldn't see his family just once more, and have another chance to fly high in the sky with his children, grandchildren and great grandchildren but if it wasn't to be it wasn't to be.

The only fear he had was being drawn into conflict with the trolls.

An Alternative Approach

Belman sat in his apartment in the Monolith administration building. His usually smiling face wore a mask of concern as he spoke to Landsman who sat opposite him.

"Don't you see Landsman, that this time we must take a completely different approach? The guilds have never been particularly subtle in war. They have always just rushed out and set upon us as soon as we show our faces. The trouble is they are very good at it. Those dwarves are maniacs. They have to be to fight the way they do.

"All the more reason to put a big force out in the field then. This time they wont be able to tear into us the way they have done in the past. If we can get fifty thousand good, well armed trolls around Aspic it will just fall before us irrespective of their sorcerer. And this time, as Dustman keeps saying, we have the support of a dragon"

"Don't remind me. I know what Dustman says about the dragon, but I think it can do us as much damage as it will them. We don't have anyone with the old skills of dragon speech and I don't know if we can control that beast at all. It seems quite benign just lying there in the field but once it gets up and starts walking who knows where it will end up."

"But it would divert their attention long enough for us to get our forces to surround Aspic. Their sorcerer won't be able to stop us then.

"But apart from the dragon as a diversion, isn't that what we have always done in the past? And hasn't it always been a failure? We have to try a new approach. The first step was to get the clans to agree to a force being formed from members of each clan. Now, if we can mould these trolls into fifty thousand well trained units of one troll which can fight and survive on its own, then we can eat the guilds."

"Don't say things like that. It makes me think of this sorcerer they have hired. What do you think they feed him on, their own people, young animals, or what?"

"Does it really matter? All we know is that he is there and we have to find a way of fighting the guilds without exposing ourselves to the sort of massacre which we have suffered too often on occasions past. I think we can do it like this."

Bellman produced a map of Midland and began to sketch out his ideas for Landsman. It was the first time he had seriously discussed it with anybody.

"Look, in the past we have always made straight for Aspic because anything smaller then a major force would be flattened by the opposition. They have no logical approach to war and have always followed a philosophy of hit first and think, if at all, much later. We, on the other hand, have been so bound up in the tradition of the journey that we have never taken the time to sit and think how best to overcome this sort of reaction. It was only the fact that we sent out some exploratory parties that enabled them to get any intelligence at all."

Landsman looked more and more worried as Bellman outlined his new ideas. The wars had always been fought to the same pattern in the past and, being conservative like most trolls, Landsman did not hold with a lot of sudden breaks in tradition. Bellman had only one major item in favour of his ideas. The traditional way did not work.

After listening to Bellman for another five minutes he said, "Well your idea seems simple enough if I understand it properly. We send out a number of small well armed, well trained groups of trolls. They have to go around the country destroying crops, breaking down bridges and generally being a thorough nuisance. Then, when the guilds are in complete disarray, which they will be because they will try to send all their forces after each of the groups we send, then we march straight up through Midland without waiting to capture any of the cities. Is that right?"

"Broadly speaking, yes."

"What if it doesn't confuse them? Or we can't find any bridges to burn or crops to destroy?"

"Well of course we will. And we shall be able to. If we start asking what if, we could terrify ourselves. What if the guilds find a way of fighting dragons. What if their sorcerer thinks of a way of unburning bridges or crops? The possibilities are endless if we take that approach. You mark my words Landsman, if we adopt this approach to fighting we have the best ever chance of completing the journey. The only problem I have is that I need your support every step of the way. Without it, if we get underway, it will break down half way through and we will be worse off than ever."

"Okay Bellman. You seem to be certain of what you are doing. I will support you. But one thing please. Don't ask me to justify your ideas to other clansmen. I'd probably end up in the asylum."

"There's no fear of that my friend. You just vote with me in the council and I will do the talking. As for now I've kept you here too long already. You go along home and think about it. I will see you in council tomorrow."

The two trolls rose and Bellman saw his guest to the door. Having made their farewells Landsman headed for home. Bellman stepped back into his apartment, picked up his cloak, pulled it about him and made his way out of the building. It was just dusk but by the time Bellman had walked the half mile to his destination it was quite dark. His journey ended at a tavern. It was a large dark stone building which had nothing to recommend it to the casual observer, except possibly the brewer's sign which was fixed, askew, to the wall beside the main door. Bellman pushed the door and went in.

The inside of the inn was as unsavoury as the outside and any of Bellman's friends who saw him enter such a place would have been surprised that he knew of it, never mind frequented it. He walked through one large dingy room in which some roughly dressed trolls were drinking from large coarsely finished flagons. He passed through a much smaller room which housed a pair of old trolls throwing knives at a target on the door.

Without appearing to notice them Bellman opened the target door and walked into a third room. It was much warmer and brighter once in the room and there was a buzz of conversation in the place which stopped as soon as Bellman entered. A group of three trolls sitting in one corner looked closely at Bellman then one of them rose from his seat .

"It's only old Bindle. 'Salright lads, he's with us. Come on Bindle old son, sit down and get yerself outside of a beer."

As Bellman sat down at the table the conversation began again. Slowly at first but by the time he had a drink it was back at the original level.

"You took a chance.... coming here chief, didn't you? This lot would stomp you into the ground if they knew who you were."

"Well fortunately they don't so I'll thank you not to mention it any further, I wouldn't have come here if it wasn't important so get four more beers and listen to an idea I need your help with."

Some more drinks were ordered and the four chatted idly while they waited. The monotony was briefly broken when a scuffle broke out between two trolls on the other side of the room. They rolled around the room for a while, kicking, punching and pulling at each other, and would have continued but for the barman kicking both of them as he passed with the four beers, and telling them to either stay in and drink or get out and fight. The two got up from the floor and elected to drink just as they had done most other nights for the last few years. Bellman and his companions turned their attention to their drinks and conversation.

"Last time you went to the Midlands you saw what you think was the guild's hired sorcerer and you tried to capture him.

"Yes."

"That's right."

"Uncommon big he was."

"Well at that time I thought it was a mistake but I've been thinking about it and on reflection I think it was a good idea. I want you to go back and try again. But this time I want more than the sorcerer, I want the guildsmen who are negotiating with him."

"What for Chief?"

"Uncommon difficult."

" Don't start all that again. Just listen. I'm not too worried how you do it but I want this sorcerer brought here to Monolith before we begin the journey proper."

"It could be expensive Bellman. Who is going to pay for it?"

"The clan funds can run to it. And if it works we can charge the whole exercise up to the journey fund. If not then we just shut up and pretend it never happened."

The three trolls nodded agreement and Bellman finished his drink. The agents were not much to work with but they were all he had. On the basis that something was better than nothing he would send them out into the field. Ulric, the leader, could cope with most situations given time. Osric, his number two provided moral support and, more importantly, could control Malvo, the third troll in the team. Malvo could not think very well and did not remember orders for more than an hour or two, but he was a ferocious fighter and could always be called upon not to desert the other two in the case of an attack.

"That's settled then," said Bellman, pulling a pouch of gold from his belt.

"Take this gold to cover expenses and report back to me personally whatever happens. Oh, and by the way, try not to damage the sorcerer. I need him in working order."

Bellman rose from the table and made his way to the door, pausing momentarily to make sure the knife throwers in the next room did not pin him to the door by his ears, he pushed his way through the crowd and out into the night. The pieces were beginning to fall into place.

The Inspection

Axel was getting worried. The Guilds had been making preparations for ten days and as yet there was no sign of any further activity from the trolls. He had enquired of his agents all over Midland but nothing had been seen of the trolls or dragons since the expeditionary force had been wiped out. He taxed Miko with the problem at least once each day.

Mike, for his part, was treating the delay as a benefit to be used for further preparation. This did not go down at all well with the negotiating committee. On the tenth day after Mike's appointment as Commander-in-Chief of the fighting forces the whole committee cornered him.

"Look Miko," said Axel, in a mildly agitated manner, "Its not that we don't believe you. It's just that things do not feel right. The trolls have not come out of the troll gate and that can only mean one thing. They must be preparing a gargantuan force for a huge attack on Aspic."

"That's not all Miko," Added Bandor, "If the dwarves don't get some action pretty soon they'll be cutting each others heads off or using their new crossbows for elf baiting. Something has to be done."

"Well what do you suggest we do? Go into Southend and pull the trolls out by the scruffs of their neck. I can't magic trolls up out of nowhere."

"Why not," asked Esmeralda. "You are supposed to be a sorcerer."

"How many more times do I have to tell you that I'm not a sorcerer. I'm an engineer."

"Yes Miko, we all know about that, but only a sorcerer of the highest order could have come up with that spell for a crossbow. That really is something."

"Alright, alright" sighed Mike, looking for way of changing the subject. "I'll see what I can do but first I have to inspect the work we have done so far. That means that I want to inspect a random selection of fighting camps and to visit Aspic." He added under his breath "That should keep you occupied for a few days while I think of something else."

"Excellent," said Axel. "Esmeralda will get you a broom."

"No she will not," retorted Mike, whose experiences with brooms were limited but terrifying. "As official sorcerer I reserve the right to use my own transport."

"But Miko," They all chorused, "It will take days if you use your own transport."

"I know it will, but at least I shall be able to work at sorcering while I am travelling."

They argued for a while but Mike's adamant refusal to use anything other than the Land Rover finally prevailed. They eventually agreed an itinerary that would get Mike to three fighting camps, a supply depot and Aspic in a period of four days; Mike hoped it would give him enough time to think of some further tactic to satisfy the committee.

Once that was settled Mike pressed his advantage and asked each of the others to review the status of their projects. The results were quite pleasing. The dwarves were set up in small camps containing no more than ten thousand individuals in each. Bandor had, at Mike's suggestion, instituted a training programme of unarmed combat to enable the dwarves to stay interested in the project without killing or maiming each other. The results had been spectacularly successful. The dwarves were worked up to fever pitch according to Bandor and the injuries had been limited to a few broken heads and legs,

The supply problem had been well covered by Leander who had managed to find a number of storage locations that were practically unreachable by a large attacking force. They were also capable of supporting the dwarves in the field or providing secondary supplies to the main towns without having long convoys of brooms strung out across the country. One of the major surprises to Mike had been that brooms traveled at ground level. According to Axel the cost of charging them to travel more than two yards above the ground was astronomical just in terms of the 'Eye of Newt' required. Wilberforce and Lutetia had continued to do a remarkable job of procuring supplies which Mike felt must have bordered on the illegal. The dwarves had been kitted out with crossbows and bolts and had proved quite adept at handling them.

Axel had used the time to set up an intelligence gathering network with contacts in all parts of Midland. He had one room at the University which had been set aside for the collection of messages and one could see curious looking characters appearing and disappearing at all hours of the day and night. It had amazed Mike than nobody had a serious accident.

All in all Mike was satisfied that the guilds were better prepared than they had any right to be. He hoped to verify his thoughts by his trip in the Land Rover.

On the morning of the eleventh day Mike set out in the Land Rover to inspect the state of his forces. He had with him Wilberforce, to keep him pointed in the right direction, and an empty seat which would occasionally be filled by somebody wanting the answer to a question. It had worried him at first the way people kept appearing out of thin air, but he managed to get used to it eventually.

Wilber guided him south initially to a dwarf camp near Broomgrove. As they made the final approach to the place Bandor appeared in the seat beside Mike. "Now Miko, this is camp full of crack fighting dwarves. They expect their commanders to be fierce and aggressive. See what you can do for them. "

Mike drove to the centre of the camp and stopped the Rover. As he climbed out he was surrounded by a milling rabble of dwarves all pushing and shoving to get a closer look at him. He heard snippets of their conversation.

"Doesn't look much does he?"

"Bit of a dog's breakfast if you ask me,"

"I wonder if all sorcerers look as daft as that."

He was sure that something should be done, but was not sure what. At that point someone put a foot in front of Mike's and he fell sprawling to the ground. He turned to find one dwarf laughing much too loudly at his discomfort. Some manners needed to be taught where Generals were concerned.

In a blind fury Mike picked himself up and caught the dwarf a long swinging blow with the back of his clenched fist. The dwarf looked momentarily stunned but recovered quickly enough to avoid Mike's follow through with a left hook to his jaw. Mike continued to advance on the dwarf who crouched low looking for an opportunity to get under Mike's arms. When the opportunity arose the dwarf came driving in with his head down, aiming for Mike's midriff. He might have made it but for Mike's knee which came up by reflex and caught his opponent under the jaw. The dwarf stood looking glazed for a moment and then prepared to come in again, Mike stood watching the dwarf's eyes for some indication of an attack. As he watched the eyes crossed briefly and then closed. The dwarf sank unconscious to the floor and a great shout went up from the crowd. Mike was picked up and carried on dwarfish shoulders all around the camp.

When he left the camp Mike was in no doubt of the spirit of the forces as far as the approaching fight was concerned. They were all looking forward to a good rumble. As he drove away with Wilber and Bandor Mike looked at his skinned knuckles.

"What did that oaf want to trip me up for?"

" He didn't."

"Well if he didn't want to, why did he do it?"

"No Miko," said Bandor, "I mean he didn't trip you up."

"Do you mean I attacked the wrong Dwarf?"

"Oh no. You attacked the right one. It just wasn't him that tripped you."

"Who was it then?"

"Does it really matter Miko. The fact is that you demolished one of their better fighters and made an excellent impression."

"But who tripped me up Bandor? Mike's voice had a curious rising inflection which members of his family would have recognised as a prelude to violence.

"It was a dwarf ."

"But which Dwarf?" Still that rising inflection.

"Uh..   It   was   me." Mike stamped on the brake and tried to reach for Bandor's throat. All he got was a handful of fresh air as Bandor disappeared. For the umpteenth time Mike wished he could do that trick.

As Mike and Wilber continued their journey to the next dwarf encampment Mike began to see the humour of the situation. He hoped Bandor would not want him to fight at every camp. They had to travel for another two hours to reach the next camp and as they traveled Esmeralda suddenly appeared in the seat beside Mike.

"Bandor asked me to make you promise not to attack him if he comes back."

"Doesn't sound like Bandor, to back off a fight that is."

"Oh he's not worried about the fight. It's just that he feels honour bound not to retaliate in case he damages you. Therefore he would rather not fight at all. If you were anybody else he would not worry about it."

"Okay," said Mike, "It's nice to know that rank has its privileges, even here".

Esmeralda disappeared and Bandor replaced her. He was pleased to see Mike smiling but he did not say anything until they were inside the camp. Even then he kept the conversation to the minimum necessary. Word of Mike's fight had already reached the local camps so there was no need for him to repeat the performance. Instead he spent most of his time in the armoury. As they left the arrow store Mike's conversation with the local dwarves was drowned by a sudden crescendo of voices which blossomed all around them. This was followed by a brief pause and then the sound of running feet. Then a dwarf ran past them shouting.

"Trolls, We've found trolls. Everybody out. Let's go. Let's go."

Mike watched with amazement as every dwarf in the place broke into a run. It was as much as he could do to fight his way through the throng to Bandor and hold him back.

"Where are these trolls?" he demanded.

"About ten leagues to the south,"

"Well why are we running down to them, There must be two other camps between us and them. How many trolls were seen '?"

"Who counts trolls? We're just going to go down and bash them."

"Do you mean that all my talking has been wasted'?"

"Of course not. A day's good march, then an hours rest. Then we lacerate them with the crossbows you made for us."

"No, not that. I mean that everybody is running after one set of trolls. We are committing all our resources. What if another lot turns up here after you've gone? What if the first lot are just a decoy?"

"Then we all run back again."

Mike could not continue the conversation. He was disappointed, frustrated and annoyed. He watched the dwarves pouring out of the camp. They all moved easily, carrying their normal armaments and the extras which he had supplied.

He was surprised at the ease with which they formed a long running column. He had heard that fighting dwarves were not easily tired but had never seen more than fleeting evidence. Within ten minutes the camp was silent and empty save for the sound of a few older, unfit dwarves who went around making the place secure.

'Well at least they seem good at what they do,' he thought, 'Even if it is the wrong thing.' "Come on Bandor," he added aloud, "we might as well tag along and see this fight."

"Surely Miko, we must, but I can't wait for you. As a guild representative I claim the right to use my own transport." And suddenly Bandor was not there. Mike thought once again that he really should learn that trick.

Mike found Wilberforce cowering in one of the large tents which the dwarves had erected. He had no wish to see the fighting at all. It took all Mike's persuasion to stop him going straight back to the University without showing Mike the way. In the end Mike had to point out that the penalty for running out on the most powerful sorcerer in the land could be something very nasty, particularly if that sorcerer was loony. Wilber's fear of the known finally overcame his fear of the unknown.

"Come on then," said Mike, "Let's get to this fight before one side demolishes the other. I want to see how the trolls shape up."

"Alright Miko. But I think you should know that I am not very good at fighting and if I am killed it will all be your fault."

"Don't worry Wilber," Mike said as he climbed aboard the Land Rover. "Who's going to kill you when you have my protection?"

They drove off in silence.

When Mike and Wilber reached the battle scene the fight was in full swing. The trolls appeared to be fielding about five thousand bodies and a large pack of ugly ferocious dogs sporting spiked collars. The dogs were being harassed by a large group of dwarves with crossbows. It was obvious to Mike that the dwarves would ultimately win if only because of superior fire power. There were ten thousand of them surrounding the trolls and Mike knew of twice that number who were on their way to help. One thing which puzzled Mike was the way the dwarves used the crossbows only against the dogs. When engaged against the trolls they reverted to clubs and axes which were also the main weapons of the trolls.

As near as Mike could work out the trolls had been surprised whilst looking for one of the supply dumps which Leander had set up in the area. They were now pinned down in a ring of trees but seemed to be giving a good account of themselves. The pile of injured and maimed seemed to be ninety percent dwarfish.

After some time spent in observation Mike caught sight of Bandor in direct combat with a troll. Each had a large club and was trying to remove the head of the other with a single sweeping blow. Mike grabbed the nearest passing dwarf and asked how he could get Bandor out of the fray for just a few moments. The dwarf said nothing but immediately ran into the fight and stood alongside Bandor hitting the troll. For about two minutes the dwarf's attention was more on their conversation than the fight but they finally reached some sort of agreement and the second dwarf came back to Mike's side and said that Bandor would be out in just a moment. Mike turned his attention back to the fight. Bandor had really turned on his aggression and Mike could see why the thickset man had such a fearsome reputation. The troll, on the other hand, was not immediately overcome by Bandor's attack. The net effect was merely to speed up the action.

Eventually however Bandor's attack became so fast and furious that the troll was driven to the ground under a rain of blows each of which was fatal in Mike's estimation. When Bandor left, however, the troll was climbing shakily to his feet to carry the fight to another waiting dwarf.

"Miko, glad you could get here before it's all over. It won't be long now."

The dwarf was not even panting. "These trolls must have been training though. They haven't fought this well in years. Look at that big fellow down there by the tree. This could be one of the best rumbles in recent history."

"But Bandor, you have up to thirty thousand dwarves committed to this tiny group of trolls. There can't be more than five thousand of them even with their pack of hounds. At this rate, with fifty thousand trolls, they could tear us to pieces."

"But trolls wouldn't be that subtle, they always throw everything they have at us."

"Having seen the way you fight I am not surprised. You're all mad. I wouldn't take you on without a ten to one advantage,"

Before Bandor could respond another dwarf appeared out of thin air beside him.

"More trolls," he gasped, "Over twenty leagues to the north."

Bandor thought for a moment before reacting. Mike thought it one of the most encouraging sights he had witnessed that day.

"Take the forces from the Gloom Wood camp and from those surrounding Aspic but don't take any more. The trolls seem to be departing from tradition."

The guild dwarf did not hear most of it as he had disappeared after the initial instruction.

Bandor turned to Mike. I don't like this very much Miko. It looks as though you might be right."

"Of course I'm right. I'm a sorcerer."

"I know but I don't have to like it."

"Alright Bandor but you should not be here. As General in charge of fighting you should be back at the University directing the forces."

"I suppose you're right," said Bandor and without further ado he disappeared leaving Mike and Wilber in the middle of a pitch battle for which they both felt ideally unqualified. Mike leapt aboard the Rover and Wilber needed no further encouragement to jump into the passenger seat. As they drove away the dwarves began to get the upper hand and by the time they were half way back to Westown the battle was over.

Intelligence

Ulric, Osric and Malvo, like most trolls, could pass for men if they had to. It was only in the context of large groups that trolls were strikingly different from men. An anthropologist might have said that they filled the gap between dwarves and men. Few of them stood more than five feet nine inches and most had very deep, well muscled chests.

They were physically very hard but none of these characteristics were very evident until a group of some ten trolls stood together. Then the effect was obvious. Three trolls in a group of men could easily pass a casual inspection.

Using the cover of night the three had slipped out of Monolith just ahead of the fighting forces which Bellman had convinced the council to send into Midland. They had reached the troll gate easily in a day and had rested there overnight before beginning the four day journey to Westown. The four days march did not concern them in the least. Their major problem was how to catch a sorcerer.

They had seen this one in action and were sure he would not give up easily. They had thought of just overpowering him but Malvo, whose judgement was trusted in all things physical, had said that overpowering such a determined opponent would very probably damage him which was against Bellman's express instructions. This aspect of their task continued to worry them.

"We could net him." Ulric suggested.

"How do we carry a net that big around Westown without being suspected of something suspicious?" replied Osric.

As usual most of the conversation was between the two of them with Malvo's remarks being confined the degree of unusualness of various aspects of the day's activity.

"Well what about a rope. Then we could tie him up if we find him."

"And how does carrying a large length of rope support our story of being merchants from Aspic?"

"Well you think of something."

"Unusually hard it is."

"Thank   you   Malvo." The conversation followed this sort of pattern for the whole of the four days. The group reached no conclusion whatever except that Malvo became more convinced than ever of the relative difficulty of catching a sorcerer.

When the trio reached Westown they made their way to a small inn, which it had been their habit to use on previous visits to the town. The landlord had an interest in money bordering on the lunatic. He would do almost anything for it including letting rooms to strange characters who could have lived more cheaply elsewhere had anybody trusted them enough to give them a room. His basic philosophy was that if people were prepared to pay his prices then he would not ask them why. The three trolls preferred the place because they were able to catch up on all the criminal gossip around the place. The sign outside the inn bore a picture of a stag in full flight beneath which was the legend 'The Fast Buck'.

Inside the three companions settled themselves for a peaceful evening's drinking at the bar. Their main purpose was to sit and listen to the other people in the place. They kept up a slight patter of idle conversation and, at infrequent intervals, bought drinks for a stranger who might have some useful information. The news of the sorcerer was scarce. Everybody knew that he had been hired but what he was doing, or where, seemed to be unknown. The one thing they did find out was that the centre of the guild's defence was the university.

Ulric decided that they would have to find out a little more before they could act. He suggested this to the others.

"Okay Ulric, but what are Malvo and I going to do?"

"The two of you can wait here until I return. By then I might some sort of plan."

"But what if you don't get a plan? If we're cut off or suchlike? Left on our own?"

"Of course I'll get a plan."

"Well I don't like it. I think we should stick together."

"Very well then. But remember, we have to look like three ordinary citizens."

"Well we are ordinary citizens. At least I am."

"Not here we're not. Now let's drink up and get some sleep. We need to be sharp witted tomorrow."

"Unusually sharp witted." added Malvo.

They finished their drinks and retired. While the other two slumbered deeply Ulric slept only fitfully. In his heart he did not feel cut out for cloak and dagger work.

In the morning, feeling worn and a little hung over, the agents of Monolith set out for the University. Although they knew their way about the city quite well it took them twenty minutes to walk there. They arrived at the square through which Mike had first entered. Once inside they sat at the bar. They were very good at sitting at bars.

After half an hour of watching a few people of all descriptions doing very little they were becoming dejected.

"Unusually quiet." offered Malvo

"I hope something happens soon."

"I told you both to stay at the inn."

"I know you did but I.. Wait a bit. What's going on over there?"

The whole of the yard seemed to erupt into activity. There were men, dwarves and elves running all over the place tripping over Faeries, Gnomes and Pixies. In no time at all, the bar was full of questions with very few available answers. Where are they? How many are there? Do they have dragons ?". As suddenly as the noise of the crowd had sprung up, it died down. About four yards in front of the trolls a tall man in pointed hat was speaking to the crowd in general.

"It seems that we have found some trolls and a force of dwarves has been dispatched to deal with them. At the moment I have no more news but Miko the sorcerer is on his way back and when he arrives he should be able to give you some idea of where things stand."

As soon as he finished the babble of questions boiled over the quadrangle again.

"There," said Ulric, in a low voice. "I told you I'd come up with a plan. All we have to do is wait here until he arrives, then we nab him."

"How do we do that in front of all these people?"

"I don't know yet but we'll find a way. We've come this far after all and I'm not going to be put off now that we are in sight of the quarry."

"What quarry?" asked a puzzled Malvo. "I don't see any quarry."

"Go back to sleep," said Ulric and Osric together.

The three trolls waited quietly for several hours before Mike put in an appearance. He arrived at the square in a flurry of dust. He had no time to get out of the Rover but was immediately surrounded by enquirer's wishing to know what they should do. He finally had no choice but to jump on the back of the Rover and shout at them.

"The trolls have begun their attacks but from what I have been told they are departing from their normal patterns. They are attacking in small groups and hitting important targets. I suggest that you all lend a hand to set the final city defences in position."

Axel fought his way through the crowd to speak to Mike.

"Miko, thank goodness you're back. The trolls are hitting us everywhere at once. They are not doing much real damage to our forces but they are damaging a lot of important equipment. They've never done anything like this before. The dwarves are coping with it but it's driving them mad not knowing where to run to the next fight. From all the bits and pieces I have it seems that there are small groups of trolls operating all over the place with instructions to do as much damage as possible. I've just been told they've destroyed the bridge over the river Aspic."

"That means they have no forces this side of the river and they don't expect us to get reinforcements to our forces on the other side very quickly. If we can repair that bridge then we can surprise them and put their forces in disarray."

"But Miko, that bridge has stood there for years. The spell was cast by a sorcerer centuries ago. Nobody remembers the spell he used."

"But aren't I, Miko, the greatest sorcerer in the west. I'll make up a new spell as I go along. I'll have to have all my equipment with me. That means loading up with all the stuff I unloaded when I arrived." Mike looked around the square and saw what he wanted beside the bar, three large, strong men who looked as though they knew bow to lift without damaging themselves or their load.

"Hey you three," he called out, "don't just sit there. Come over here and I'll tell you what you can do to help the war effort."

Ulric, Osric and Malvo approached the Land Rover and Mike gave them precise instructions where to find the things he was after, mainly his surveying apparatus, and threatened them with dire consequences if they damaged any of it. They disappeared, mumbling.

"Who were they" asked Axel.

"I don't know but I've seen them before around here," Mike replied. "I just hope they won't object to coming to the bridge with me. I'm going to need some strong men.

When the three trolls returned with his gear Mike told them where it should be stored and then called Axel and the trolls to a brief conference. Axel, for no reason that he could identify, did not like the three newcomers however Mike brushed his comments aside and suggested that the three accompany himself and Wilberforce to the site of the destroyed bridge. There they should be able to make the necessary repairs and get dwarf forces over the river to surprise the troll forces returning to Southend. In view of the potential hazard of the journey he was delighted at the willingness of his three new helpers. He was not surprised at the total unwillingness of Wilberforce who had to be placed bodily in the Rover and made to swear that he would not run out on the trip.

To add weight to the arguments Axel told the goblin in a very grave voice "You must accompany Miko on this trip. After all, he should always have a guild negotiator with him who can advise him of guild practices and keep him in check if he tries any spells which are too wild."

If this was intended to make Wilber feel any better it produced the opposite effect. His face grew longer by the minute. In the end he sat in the Land Rover in complete silence with a look of total desolation on his face. Mike would have excused him from the duty had he been able to navigate unaided. Unfortunately he could not so Wilber had to make the best of it.

Ulric wore a grin like a jackass. The more Mike and Axel said the better it seemed. Instead of having to find the sorcerer and capture him they were being handed him on a plate. Instead of having to find a guild negotiator they were to be accompanied by one and instead of having to drag them back by their hair they were being transported most of the way. And by a shorter route to boot.

Osric smiled contentedly. He had no idea what Ulric was going to do but he had absolute faith. He would just wait for Ulric to call the play and then he would do what was required.

Malvo had no idea about anything. He could not see why they were about to ride off on a strange conveyance instead of just bashing the sorcerer over the head and running off with him. He decided to wait for the instruction to bash somebody.

With the three trolls on the back of the Rover, Wilber in the passenger seat and a feeling of mounting excitement Mike set off to the burned bridge. As they traveled he tried to engage his new companions in conversation but the difficulty of talking over his shoulder proved too much with the unresponsive group in the back. Most of the journey was conducted either in silence or with Mike singing. The only other interruption was an occasional strangled cry from Wilber telling Mike which path to follow.

When they eventually arrived at the river the situation had to change.

Mike needed assistance and, to some extent, advice. It took him a couple of hours with his surveying gear to devise a way of reinstating the bridge but he had to obtain the necessary materials. In this the trolls and Wilber were invaluable.

After telling them the type of thing he required they suggested either alternatives or easily available sources. By the evening Mike had all the lumber he required stacked at the site of the bridge, mainly due to the remarkable abilities of the three trolls who had carried most of it manually from the forest after cutting it.

The biggest problem had been axes. Wilber had refused point blank to go back to the school because he would either be accused of leaving Mike unguarded or would be unable to find the courage to return. In the end the trolls had fashioned some very creditable surrogates from a couple of pieces of steel which had been lying in the back of the Rover. This had impressed Mike. It was the first indication he had seen of any degree of mechanical inventiveness. When he taxed the trolls with this their only response had been a non-committal shrug of their broad deep shoulders.

That evening they sat round a fire which Mike had started with the battery and petrol technique, thereby terrifying the trolls. He spent a lot of time mulling over his luck in finding three such strong, willing workers. There was definitely something strange about them but he could not identify what it was and fell asleep thinking about it.

In the morning, awakened and fresh, Mike put his mind and his back into the task of refurbishing the destroyed bridge. With the aid of the trolls, Wilberforce being no use whatever, he made short work of the task. By mid afternoon he was able to stand in the middle of the structure and survey his handiwork. Whilst it was true that the river was only some twenty yards across, and much of the original structure had escaped destruction, he felt pleased with the elegance of the finished solution compared with the old one. Admittedly he did not have all the tables he would have liked for his calculations of beam size and he had taken a few chances with his memory, but on the whole he was happy that the renewed structure was both sound and pleasing to the eye.

"There it is," he said to his companions, to whom that much was already obvious. "What do you think of it?" Wilber, who was overcome with admiration, could only nod with a mixture of fear at Miko's power and relief that the task had been completed without sight of trolls.

Ulric looked a trifle concerned.

"It looks good Miko," he said with a doubtful look in his eye, "but are you sure it's strong enough."

"Of course it's strong enough. My spells don't pack up after a week. This bridge will last for years."

"Well if you say so, but I reckon you must have put some sort of extra powerful spell on that middle section where we used the short spars, otherwise it'll just collapse as soon as someone goes over it with a heavy load."

"Of course it won't, anyway who's the engineer here? You or me? I'll show you how much weight it will stand. All jump in the Rover."

A big grin spread over Ulric's face as Mike said this. Things were going very well. If he could just get the sorcerer and his transport over the bridge he could, at last, show his hand.

Mike drove the Rover, with a full complement of men and equipment, very carefully over the first half of the bridge and stopped in the centre. The track of the bridge was about two feet wider than the Rover and when he stopped Mike leaped out of the driving seat and began to jump up and down on the bonnet. Wilber sat in the passenger seat and shivered. He was terrified of ending up in the river. Mike climbed back into the driving seat and put the Land Rover into reverse.

"There," he shouted in triumph, "That should convince you." He began to slowly back off of the bridge.

Ulric was on the verge of panic. There would never be a better opportunity to get the sorcerer to the other side of the river but until they were actually off of the bridge on the far side he dare not exert force. He tried desperately to think of a way to get Mike over the bridge. Wilber saved him the trouble.

"Miko, for pity's sake. It's bad enough that you bring us all out here on this strange broom of yours but please don't go driving it backwards. Just for me would you please go over the bridge, turn around and come back forwards."

Mike laughed. There was no point in frightening Wilber too much. He might lose his way. He threw the Rover into forward gear and drove smoothly over the bridge. As he slowed down Ulric jumped unbidden out of the back.

"Hold on Miko, I think heard something giving." Osric and Malvo jumped out after him sensing that something was about to happen. Ulric ushered them to the riverbank where they were out of Mike's earshot.

"Keep looking at the bridge while I call him over. When he gets here we turn and overpower him."

Mike climbed out of the Rover, closely followed by Wilberforce who was in a state of severe agitation, and approached the three. Wilber was jumping at every sound and when Mike stepped on a dry twig the crack made the goblin jump almost out of his skin. When Mike was about five yards from the three trolls they turned to face him. He needed no other indication that something was wrong. The juxtaposition of the three rang alarm bells in his mind. The three massive profiles fell into place and he saw his three assailants from the alleyways of Westown.

"Trolls," he snapped. That was too much for Wilberforce who disappeared in the blinking of an eye.

Mike stood eyeing the trolls with his mind racing. He could fight and probably go down, or he could run for the Rover, but knowing the troll's speed he doubted his chances of making it. Or he could bluff it out. He was, after all, a great sorcerer as he had just proved. He might be able to negotiate some sort of peace if he took the initiative. Ulric beat him to it.

"Miko, there are three of us and one of you. It makes sense that in the long run we should be able to overpower you. We don't want to and I'm sure you don't want us to. We have orders to bring you in uninjured and I'd just as soon do it that way."

"What do you want me for?"

"Not me, my chief. He wants to talk to you."

"Where?"

"Monolith."

"What guarantees do I have?"

"None. What choice do you have?"

"None. But that doesn't usually stop me."

"I believe you Miko. You're a very powerful sorcerer. The spell you cast over that bridge is quite something. It would take our builders a long time to come up with anything half way decent. You cast that spell in a day. That should give you some sort of guarantee in itself. You are far more useful to us alive that dead. A dead sorcerer is no use to anybody."

Mike considered for a moment and then visibly relaxed. The rational argument put forward by Ulric appealed to his scientific curiosity.

"All right," he said, "I'll make a deal with you. I'll come to Monolith if you will answer my questions as we go."

"Okay Miko, but I need a couple of promises from you first. You have to promise not to attack anybody we might meet, particularly children, and you will try to act like a troll and not arouse suspicion."

"Agreed." said Mike, puzzled by the nature of the request.

"Okay. We go this way.'" and Ulric relaxed as turned to face the south. "It's about two days walk from here."

"Walk?" You must be mad. We sorcerers don't walk. That's why we have these clever transporters. Jump in and we'll be there tonight with any luck."

After some argument Ulric agreed that they could use the transporter provided that Mike was prepared to leave it outside the town and walk the last few miles. Once in the Rover Mike set off in the indicated direction. He was, in spite of himself, excited at the prospect of visiting Monolith. At last he would be able to find out something about the trouble between the trolls and the Guilds. The only concern he had was that the guilds might suffer heavy losses while he was unable to help them. He put the thought out of his mind and began asking Ulric some questions.

"Tell me, why are the trolls coming out of Southend."

"To begin the journey of course," said Ulric, puzzled.

"What journey is that?" Mike countered.

"The one we begin by leaving Southend."

"But where is this journey to, Ulric?"

"The north."

"I know that," snapped Mike. Then more carefully, "But where in the north?"

"I don't know."

"Well who does?"

"Nobody as far as I know."

"How can nobody know where you're going?" Mike snarled sensing that his conversation was an exact parallel with his Guild discussion.

"Well every time we come out of the troll gate the Guilds set on us and wipe out half our men. We've never made it further north than Treforest in living memory so how can we know where we are going?"

"So you just come out of Southend every so often, have a huge rumble with the guilds and then go home again."

"Well yes....I suppose you could say that. From our point of view every time we begin the journey we're set upon by a bunch of madmen who try to wipe us out. Mind you, they don't always succeed. Their losses are usually heavier than ours."

"From what I've seen the whole situation is preposterous. You don't know why you come out of Southend but you always do. The guilds don't know either but they attack you anyway. There must be a reason.

"You'll have to ask Bellman about that."

"Who's Bellman?"

"He's our chief."

"Senior troll," added Osric

"Unusually important he is," put in Malvo.

This outburst surprised Mike who had forgotten the existence of the passengers in the back. He spent some time reflecting on his situation and its frustrations and decided he could do nothing until he met Bellman. The party drove on in a heavy thoughtful silence.

When they reached the point where Mike, peering into the twilight, could just make out the profile of a township on the horizon, they stopped. Mike parked the Rover behind a clump of bushes and they all climbed out. "Come on," said Ulric, "We'll be in Monolith within an hour."

Counterintelligence

Having got back to the school, Wilberforce was in a worse state than when he had left Mike. He ran from building to building and from room to room looking for somebody who could help him. He wanted to find Axel, or some other member of the negotiating committee, to get advice and unburden himself.

Alternatively he would have settled for someone who knew where Axel had gone.

He could find nobody. After a while his nerves began to settle and he tried to think out the best thing to do. The major problem was to get some help to Miko and the others as quickly as possible. In the end he sat and listed in his mind all the places throughout Midland that Axel might be, then he quickly visited them. There was no sign of the tall wizard. After half an hour of intense but useless activity he decided to return to Miko by himself and observe the result of the troll attack which the sorcerer had given warning of by shouting. There was no sign of Miko, his transporter or his three companions.

In a state of weary dejection Wilber returned once again to the school. The first person he saw on his return was Esmeralda.

"Esmeralda! Praise be. I've found somebody. Miko is lost to the trolls. We have to help him. I couldn't do anything. I just ran away." Esmeralda slowed the goblin down and persuaded him to repeat his story a little more slowly.

"So you didn't see any trolls," she said, when he had finished. "Miko saw them and he told you. Then you panicked and came back here," "Yes but when I went back all trace of them was gone."

"So you went back afterward. How long after you left was that?"

"Half an hour."

"Well anything could have happened in that time. But I think it was very brave of you anyway. Where was this place?"

Wilberforce explained the location and they both transported themselves to the scene of Miko's disappearance. Esmeralda looked around for a while but could see no evidence of a major battle. She thought for a long time before she spoke again.

"We can't afford to lose Miko but at the moment we can't take Axel or Bandor away from fighting the trolls. I don't think anybody else would be much use to us. Both Axel and Bandor are due to bring a force of dwarves this way as soon as they can spare them. We'll just have to wait here and ask their advice when they arrive, I suggest that in the meantime we just....,What's that?"

She was looking intently at the ground.

"What's what?"

"This funny marking on the ground. It looks like some sort of runes but I can't make them out."

"Oh that. it's a protective pattern laid down by the Dunlops."

"Who are the Dunlops? Some sort of troll?"

"No. They are the things that keep Miko's transporter off the ground."

"I don't understand. What do you mean?"

"Well when I was bringing him into the University I happened to kick one of the things which go between the transport and the ground. Miko said to me "Don't do that. That's a brand new set of Dunlops. They protect me from Skidding, sliding and over zealous traffic cops. They're worth two hundred Bucks." At least, I think that's what he said."

"They must be very powerful indeed to be worth so many animals. Why do they lay these Runes?"

"I don't know, but they lay them everywhere. I noticed that before."

"Do you mean that we can find Miko by just by following the runes. That's incredible. No wonder he's such a powerful sorcerer if he can do things like that."

"I suppose we can. But look at them. They go off in the direction of Southend. Miko wouldn't go that way."

"Miko would do anything particularly if he was lost. For a powerful sorcerer that man needs an awful lot of looking after."

"So what do we do now?"

"Simple. We get a broom and follow him."

Wilber waited nervously while Esmeralda returned to the school for a broom which would carry the two of them. When she returned Wilber asked, "What do we do about the others?".

"Oh. I'd forgotten them. If we find Miko and he's okay then we bring him back. If he's not then we turn back and fetch the others."

Wilber was not convinced but he could not think of anything better so he just kept quiet.

They followed the tracks for some hours. At regular half hourly intervals Wilber asked if they should turn back and with equal regularity Esmeralda said no. They followed the tracks through the troll gate unchallenged and continued until at last the runes ran out in a clump of bushes.

Esmeralda and Wilberforce searched the Rover and found it undamaged as far as they could tell. With an equal mixture of fear and grim determination Esmeralda sat in the driving seat and examined their situation. They had the choice of going on or back. Going on meant travelling into town, the lights of which she could see in the black distance. Going back meant waiting for Axel or Bandor to arrive at the bridge. If they took the latter course they would accomplish nothing whereas if they went on they might just learn Miko's whereabouts and get back to the bridge. They put it to a vote and Esmeralda outvoted Wilber by threatening to burn him if they did not go on. They went on.

In two hours of stumbling over unlit, unfamiliar ground they eventually made it to the edge of the town they had seen lit up on the horizon, It was large and well laid out. They were, more than anything, surprised by the artistic nature of the designs. The buildings were very well constructed, much better than anything the Guilds had. The streets were well lighted and clean with no suggestion of the low living standards that the guilds usually associated with the trolls.

"If they have Miko where would he be held?" Wilber whimpered.

"They would probably take him to their chief wherever he might live. I suppose we should look for something like the University or the public administration buildings."

They continued to prowl the town for another fifteen minutes before they came across the building after which it was named. They stood outside looking at it for a while, trying to think of something to do. They could not think of anything. Esmeralda was about to suggest that they return to the bridge when a troll came out of the main door of the building.

"Its very late to be out ma'am." he said without looking too closely at the unusually tall woman before him. "Especially with a little one. Are you lost or something?"

Esmeralda, who had been expecting to be attacked, or at least shouted at, was taken aback by the civility of the enquiry. She tried hard to frame a reply but nothing would come from her vocal chords. The troll, thinking her to be distressed, came closer. As he did a flurry of wind caught Esmeralda's cloak and blew it back revealing her normal dress of sequined leotard and fishnet tights.

"You're not one of us," gasped the troll, beginning to realise the truth of the situation. "You're from the Guilds. HELP, HELP." he began to shout at the top of his voice. "It's the Guilds, here in Monolith."

Esmeralda was torn between amazement at the troll's reaction and a desire to blast him out of existence with a lightening bolt and return to the bridge. She did neither. The troll's shouts had brought others out of the door and they surrounded her and Wilber. Given that she and the goblin could transport themselves out of the place at any time there seemed little point in doing their disappearing act until it was absolutely necessary. Wilberforce did not think anything at all. He just followed Esmeralda's example. The pair were surrounded and taken into the brightly lit interior of the building by trolls with the biggest, sharpest axes that Wilber had ever seen.

Understanding

After Mike had parked the Rover he had been led over land to the town. It had proved deceptively near and the journey had taken less than an hour although the pace was fast and the trolls knew their way. Once within the city boundary Mike had been surprised at the evident beauty of the city visible even in the artificial light.

The lights were the first incongruity he had noticed in the whole of his time in Midland and Southend. They appeared to oil or gas burning, he could not tell which but either way they showed that the trolls had a passable knowledge of basic engineering.

Ulric and his two companions escorted Mike to a large building which, Mike estimated, stood in the middle of the town. They climbed the steps and went in. Mike stood in silence while Ulric spoke to a troll sitting at a desk inside. The troll showed them to a room off the main entrance hall. Once inside Mike was left by himself.

The room he judged to have been built for security purposes. There were no windows but two doors, one at each end of the room. Across the ceiling was a row of holes, each about four inches in diameter, at eight inch intervals. Mike could find no explanation for these.

There were several chairs in the room. Mike selected one and sat in it. As he did he realised just what a long day he had had. Osric opened the door and poked his head round it.

"Are you hungry?" he enquired with a worried look.

"Hungry? I could eat a horse."

There was a choking cry from behind Osric and the troll looked exasperated.

"You promised you wouldn't upset anybody," he snapped. "Now look what you've done." Mike looked behind the door to see a troll lying on the floor in a dead feint.

"You'll be asking for a baby to eat next. You'll have troll food and like it."

"What did I do?" said Mike. But it was too late. Osric had left and the door was closed.

Bellman was annoyed when he saw Ulric standing at the door with Malvo hovering in the background.

"What are you doing here?" he barked. "Have you given up already?"

"No chief. We've got him. He's downstairs, quiet as you like."

"Unusually quiet he is."

"Really? That's tremendous," Bellman smiled, his annoyance evaporating immediately. "I'll be down directly. Where have you put him?"

"In the security room."

"Good. Get it ready. I don't want to be left alone with a monster."

"He doesn't seem much like a monster to me chief, but you know best," And with this parting comment Ulric and Malvo left.

Mike sat in the security room waiting for his food. When it came it proved to be delicious and he dispatched a large plate of it in a very short time. When he sat back in the chair afterward he felt much better. To pass the time he turned his attention to the ceiling and the unexplained holes. As he watched them their purpose became clear. The holes began to fill with something being extruded down into the room. As it reached lower into the room it revealed itself as thick wooden poles. After ten minutes the room was neatly divided in two by a row of thick wooden staves. Whichever half Mike had chosen to stand in the other side of the room could be independently entered in complete security.

"Effective", said Mike to himself, "crude but effective".

As he said it the door on the other side of the room opened and a troll entered. Mike had never seen him before but he knew that this was the troll in charge, just by looking at him. His presence and bearing demanded attention and respect.

"You must be Bellman." Mike said.

"Yes I am. You make it your business to be well informed Miko the sorcerer,"

"No more than you do. I am, after all, the one who has been kidnapped."

Kidnapped. What does that mean? Is this another of your disgusting dietary habits?"

"What disgusting habits?"

"Eating babies, crunching on men's bones to keep your fangs in good order. I suppose the guilds were feeding you on young animals. Even they would never... well, never mind about that."

"But I do mind. I hate to tell you this but I don't eat babies, bones, small animals or any other unusual diet. I can live very comfortably on guild food or, from the sample I've just had, troll food."

"But... sorcerers always eat babies and have fangs. Show me your fangs."

Mike continued the argument for about twenty minutes before Bellman would believe that he had no fangs.

Once it was settled Bellman had the bars removed from the room.

"Well sorcerer", he said, "We seem to have been acting under a few misapprehensions about you and your like."

"It seems to me that everybody is under some misapprehension about everybody else around here.   Tell me Bellman, Why do you make the journey?"

"You are supposed to answer my questions, Miko."

"I know, but you only want to know how I have helped the Guilds and what I can do for the trolls now that you have me here."

"A very shrewd assessment on your part Miko, but why should I answer any of your questions?"

"Simply because I may be able to help you complete the journey if I know something more about it. I certainly know more about the Guilds than anybody here, and now I think I know more about the trolls than anybody in the Guilds."

"You have a point there, so I will tell you of the journey. It costs me nothing and we just might get you to co-operate." Bellman moved his chair closer to Mike's and sent a troll off for more food and something to drink. Then he settled himself more comfortably and began.

"Many years ago before the world was as it is today there were three major peoples in this land of ours. They were men, trolls and dwarves. They lived in peaceful coexistence and the world was a happy innocent place. Men were great travelers and farmers. They would walk to the bounds of the land to investigate tales of good soil or unusual sights. Trolls were builders, artisans in clay and wood, stone and metal, with skills much surpassing anything we have now. We also had an affinity for animals, to the extent that some could even communicate with dragons. Dwarves were athletes, entertainers, poets and dreamers. The three groups fitted well together and they worked happily for many years until the day somebody discovered the secret of kinetics, the ability to move from one place to another in the blinking of an eye.

The economic stability of the whole country was threatened. The secret was difficult to master and everybody wanted it. Those who could master it were able to get rich very quickly and many did just that.

As if in response to this somebody else discovered the secret of broom flight. This meant cheap effective transport was available to anybody with a small amount of gold. Those with money and vision were quick to grasp this opportunity and set up assembly lines producing cheap brooms. "Any wood you like as long as it's oak." they said. Men began to travel further afield. They met other cultures. The elves and the faerie, the goblin and the gnome. All manner of people began to appear in the land. Wealth became less evenly distributed. Some people were so poor they had to steal to survive and crime started to rear its head. The mark of anarchy fell on the land and nobody knew where it would lead.

In the midst of all this the trolls began to see some problems arising. The old skills were being forgotten. The young men were no longer happy to stay home and learn the trade of their fathers'. Skills were lost and knowledge became specialised. The troll community became worried about their own future so they did something about it.

They started by setting up groups of trolls in all manner of foreign places and telling them to learn all the local crafts. The idea was that they would pull all the knowledge gained together in one place and develop a separate troll community. They would, of course, accept anybody else provided they would obey the rules. They did this for a long time and it seemed to work well. Nobody cared if the trolls were daft enough to chase silly ideas like these. There was plenty of money for people to indulge their fancies and if the trolls did not want to join in, well more fool them.

After a while things began to go wrong. Just small things at first. Things that the troll in the street wouldn't notice. The price of batwings escalated, there was a shortage of stardust, a general reduction in the quality of rhinoceros horn and newt's eyes. The trolls looked around and said, "Now is the time to get our people together. We should begin to call in the groups which we started years ago."

First of all they found a place where all the trolls could live and then they negotiated with the owners for it. Then they built up some troll institutions and began to send for trolls to come and join in the running of the community. Then they started calling the troll groups to their new homes. Some did not want to go but most went as soon as they had the opportunity. We, here, were called back but were the victims of circumstance.

By the time our turn came inflation had reached an incredible level. We had learned lots of skills but we hadn't hoarded any material wealth. We could not afford to go and we refused to stay. The cost of broom fare was horrendous and we had only a handful of brooms in the whole community. We were very rural and transport had not been one of our priorities. So we decided to wait until we could finance a major expedition.

Time passed and the price of things went further out of control. The people were going hungry and all the brooms in the world didn't give you anything to eat. We were well off here. We had all the food we could eat and more. We tried trading with the Midlands but they just accused us of being the cause of their problems. So we just settled down to wait it out. The situation in Midland went from bad to worse. The people, no longer able to afford long distance communication, broke up into fragmented societies. The land was littered with small fiefdoms run by physically powerful leaders. After many years of isolation we tried to make the journey to our homeland. Our appearance in Midland served only to give the people a rallying point and we were attacked savagely as we tried to leave Southend. We were not expecting it and more than half our people were wiped out. We had to return here to recoup our losses before trying again.

Meanwhile in Midland the Guilds were beginning to appear. They were doing much what the trolls had done years before, that is banding together for mutual protection and development. They slowly established a constitution and a sort of free economic system which blossomed into the system they have now. They remembered nothing of the older times and you must realise that this process took nearly ten thousand years altogether, of which the middle four thousand had no civilisation at all in Midland. We never recovered and nor did they. Now, every time we poke our nose out of the door somebody tries to cut it off."

Mike sat back in amazement. He had never heard any of this from the guilds.

"Why is it that you know all this and the guilds know none of it?"

"Ah, that's a good question. If you ask the average troll in the street he'll tell you that we make the journey every hundred years or so. He won't know why we do it but he will know that we fight the Guilds. I have put a lot of this together from research here in Monolith. We have an excellent library."

Bellman paused for a moment looking wistfully into space.

"It's taken me years to get the council to accept my views on the way we should respond to the threat from the guilds. This is the first time we have ever put self-sufficient units in the field. They won't be back until they have created havoc in the Guild's defenses."

"You're a bit out of luck there Bellman," Mike said. "I assumed that anybody attacking Midland would take that approach and planned accordingly, so all we've done between us is maintain the status quo."

"Well that may be good in the long run. You see, we don't want to harm the guildsmen we just want to pass them. Once we get to the top of the land we can make the journey across the sea by broom. It's very short."

"What journey across the sea?," Mike asked.

"Our journey to the troll lands of course."

"Why not go all the way by broom then?"

"Have you any idea what that would cost? Well let me just say that if we turned all our resources to making brooms we could afford about one charged broom for every twenty people. You see we still don't have any natural resources apart from food."

"Why don't you try negotiating with the Guilds?"

"You've seen what the Guilds think of trolls. If we sent a negotiating group how far do you think they would get? They'd be cut to pieces before they were half a day out of the troll gate."

"I suppose that's true."

Mike and Bellman sat looking at each other for a couple of minutes in perfect silence. Each tried to get behind the eyes of the other, to evaluate the trustworthiness and opposition. Mike broke the silence.

"What would it be worth if I could find a way of letting your people complete the journey?"

"A great deal if you could do it."

"And if I could restore some sort of working relationship with the guilds?"

"That would be worth less at the moment but could be of even greater value in the long run."

"How long do you need to spend at the top of the land?"

"I really do not know. We've never been there before so we may have to start from scratch when we get there. I'd rather assumed that once we establish a base we could explore until we found the land we were looking for. But why should you help us Miko? You seem entertaining and personable enough for a sorcerer and I quite like what I've seen of you so far, but you are being paid by the Guilds. And from what I have heard they are getting excellent value for money. Why should I trust you?"

"I can't think of one good reason from your point of view. Except that I might just be able to do what I just suggested."

Bellman frowned, His conscience urged him to go ahead and trust Mike but his years of experience held him back. Then his face slipped into its customary smile.

"My instinct tells me to trust you Miko, but my experience tells me not to. How would you council me to act?"

"Well both of your present advisors seem to have excellent qualifications. I, however, would go for my instincts. Not because it's any more likely to be right, but if you are right it's a wonderful feeling.

"And if I'm wrong?"

"If you're wrong in either case you'll feel rotten."

"You may have something there," laughed Bellman, "You just may have something there."

Bellman's laughter was cut short by the sound of scuffling and shouting outside. The door opened and a square troll head appeared from behind it. "Excuse me Bellman. I think we need your advice."

"What is it?"

The troll head looked at Mike and then, after a brief pause said,

"We've got a Guilds representative out here. She's threatening all sorts of dire things if we don't free somebody named Miko. She's also demanding to talk to you. I think she could be quite dangerous."

"You'd better send her in then. As soon as possible, before she does any damage to council property."

A group of trolls managed to hustle Esmeralda into the room without actually touching her. Then they stood around managing to look both terrified and fearsome at the same time. Esmeralda, for her part, looked both furious and tearful, as she had when Mike had been unable to transport himself back to the school. She looked somewhat the worse for wear in that her cloak was awry and her tights were wrinkled.

"Miko," she gasped, "Thank goodness. Are you okay? They haven't tortured you have they? How are we going to get you out of this? Wilberforce is outside."

"Alright Esmeralda, slow down. There's no need to panic. Let me introduce you to Bellman."

"Delighted to meet you," said Bellman, who was, in fact, rather frightened.

"You are the first Guild representative we have had here in Monolith."

"Get away from me you monster." Esmeralda shrilled. "Just let me take Miko back with me and we'll leave straight away."

"Be careful Esmeralda," broke in Mike. "We don't want to upset these good trolls. I think it's time you and I had a serious talk." He turned to Bellman.

"If you'd just let us have a few moments to talk, with Wilberforce here, I'm sure I can sort everything out to our mutual satisfaction."

Bellman and the other trolls left the room quietly and Wilberforce was brought in. When he saw Mike he was visibly relieved.

"Miko, you're safe. Now can we leave?"

"No," snapped Esmeralda. "What's all this about Miko?"

"Well it's very simple really. I've made a deal with the trolls which I think will be to everyone's satisfaction."

"Miko, that's terrific," His companions chorused. "How did you do it? Have you convinced them that you are the most powerful sorcerer ever, and that if they come out of the troll gate once more they'll be wiped out forever? Is that it?"

"No. Not quite. I've told them that I will help them make their journey and it will be in everyone's best interest to co-operate."

"I see," said Esmeralda. "Then, when they are unawares, we set on them and wipe them out."

"NO. NO. NO." Mike shouted. "Will you get this irrational aggression out of your head? We do not set about them. We help them to go where they want to."

"And then when they get there we wipe them out." put in Wilber.

"God give me strength. NO! They don't get wiped out. They go where they want to go and everybody lives happily ever after."

"How can they do that with the trolls still about."

"The trolls will be gone."

"But where to Miko?"

"To wherever they want to go."

Esmeralda could tell that she was not going to understand. So could Mike. Her bottom lip was trembling and her eyes looked distinctly watery. Mike tried to put it as simply as possible.

"I have made a deal with the trolls that ensures that they can have what they want, without taking anything from the Guilds. We may even be able to improve the lot of the Guilds at the same time."

It was too much for Esmeralda. She broke down and sobbed.

"Miko. How could you? After all you've done for us, you've sold us out. It's not fair of you. I don't suppose you'll be happy until the whole of Midland is overrun with trolls. Well I'm not going to stand around and let you get away with that. I think it's mean and shameful. Wilberforce," she turned to face the goblin. "I think we should leave now."

Wilberforce needed no second bidding and was gone in a flash. Esmeralda faced Mike.

"I thought you were really something; a talented, humanitarian with integrity and feelings. Now I see that you are just a pretty nobody whose ambition is self centred and greedy. I came here to rescue you but I seem to have made a fool of myself. Well no more. Goodbye mister Miko the Sorcerer. I hope your deal chokes you."

Instead of disappearing in her usual silence there was a heart rending crash and a smell of burning, A bolt of lightning struck the floor beside Mike's feet and he found himself once again in a ring of fire. He leaped swiftly out of it and beat out the flames with a cloak taken from the first troll he found outside the door. Then he sat down. As he did so Bellman came running in.

"Miko, what happened?"

"We had a slight row. It seems that I'm now a lost cause for the Guilds and that you have yourself a sorcerer."

"Well, well, well. Maybe it's all for the best. Now I don't have to trust you back in Midland. You can employ your talents here in Monolith in full view of the council. And, with any luck we won't need to let loose the dragon"

"Tell me about the dragon Bellman. What do you plan to use it for?"

"You can't use a dragon for anything Miko. Dragons do what they want to do. They don't do the bidding of trolls, or men. We were just lucky enough to have one fall out of the sky when we were planning the journey. A lot of Trolls think it was an omen. That's why they want to use it as a weapon to lead the charge."

"And you don't like that idea."

"No, I don't. But I may be forced into it. I'm going to see it tomorrow. Aleric will give me a report on how we can use it. Maybe you would like to come along with me. Just to see it for yourself. It's a fearsome thing, a fully grown giant of a dragon."

Mike was too tired and shocked to think straight. He knew something had to be done but was too exhausted even to frame the question in his mind. He told Bellman that he would think better on a good night's sleep and a troll was dispatched to prepare a room for him,

Five minutes later, still numb from his treatment at the hands of Esmeralda, Mike climbed out of his clothes and into a bed. He would think about it all tomorrow. In two minutes he was fast asleep.

Encounter with a Dragon

Oriender came awake slowly from a peaceful relaxed sleep. Something was different; he could smell it in the air. He raised his head from the ground and looked sleepily around him but there was nothing immediately obvious. Oriender sniffed a few times and thought he caught it again, a tang of something strange. It was familiar but he could not identify it clearly.

He stretched his shoulders and flexed the muscles in his back and tail for a moment, then, very slowly he raised his weight on his back legs and sat up to his full height. Suddenly he dominated the whole field and the retaining fence seemed rather puny. The figures coming through the small entrance to the field suddenly began to pay more attention.

Oriender watched them and began to breathe more quickly. The difference, whatever its cause, was something to do with the trolls entering the field. He gave them his undivided attention and suddenly, to his surprise, he knew what the difference was. One of them was a sorcerer.

Mike looked at the huge beast warily as he walked with Aleric and Bellman towards the dragon. He was beginning to doubt the wisdom of his actions. He had wakened that morning full of questions after a good night's sleep. He had directed many of them at Bellman while he drove them in the Rover to the dragon pen where Bellman introduced Mike to Aleric and Aleric opened the gate to the Dragon.

"Something is upsetting him," Aleric said, as they crossed the field to the sitting dragon. "I've only ever seen him sit up once before and then he lay down again almost immediately. Something is definitely getting to him."

Mike approached the dragon directly, just to get a clear idea of his size. He looked at the tail, and the legs and then he gazed upwards into the eyes of the biggest animal he had ever seen.

Oriender saw the look in Mike's eyes and brought his head right down to Mike's level. Bellman and Aleric drew back but Mike stayed where he was.

"I think," he said slowly, "That it would be better if you two just left me with the dragon for a while. There's no need to put everybody at risk."

Aleric and Bellman agreed far too quickly and backed away as fast as was seemly, leaving Mike face to face with the dragon. Small flames crept from the dragon's nostrils and Mike was aware that he was being tested in some way. He tried not to flinch as the dragon's head moved closer to his own.

"What are you trying to tell me?" he asked, putting his hand up to stroke the green scaly snout. "Why have I disturbed you more than the others?"

Oriender looked closely at the sorcerer, sniffing and sensing him from every possible angle. It wasn't just that he was a sorcerer. There was something else about him that stirred a distant memory. It was like something from his childhood. The Sorcerer did not seem to be frightened although he was cautious. He was talking in a strange tongue which meant nothing to the dragon. And yet there was something familiar about him.

Oriender closed his eyes and tried again, without the vision of the sorcerer to interfere with his memories. He recalled his childhood in the nest, the crags and peaks of his homeland and the occasional meetings with other people from all over the world. It seemed to be something to do with those other people. Had he met the sorcerer before? It seemed unlikely. Sorcerers only lived for a hundred or so years whereas dragons lived for a thousand. Well, if it wasn't the sorcerer it must have been somebody else.

He began to shake his tail in frustration. Why could he not remember? It was the first serious signs of age. His memory was not as good as it had once been. He began to remember the times of his youth again and then he recalled his own children and the trials of bringing up a well-mannered young dragon. Just as his thoughts began to drift away from the sorcerer it came to him in a flash.

"Banshees," he thought. "This sorcerer has been in contact with Banshees." He looked closely into Mike's spirit and there, sure enough, he saw the mark of a Banshee. That explained it all.

Settling himself comfortably again Oriender found the name of O'Banion and began to call it gently.

It took about five minutes for the Banshee to arrive and even when he did he was not easily visible.

Mike was still petting the dragon and wondering how to get any further when he was startled by a voice he recognised.

"Miko, the Sorcerer," said O'Banion, "You do turn up in some weird places."

"Where are you?" Mike demanded, "What are you doing here?"

"I'm not sure you can ask those questions Miko. After all, the second one presupposes the answer to the first one. But even so I'd better tell you. Oriender the dragon called me when he discovered that we knew each other."

"You know very well what I mean O'Banion. Come out where I can see you."

"I am out Miko, I'm just not very easy to see in broad daylight. But if you look closely you should be able to get a glimpse of me just beside Oriender's head"

"Excuse me," interrupted Oriender, I know you two have met before but would you mind telling me what's going on here."

"Who's Oriender, and what made that noise?" Mike asked.

"I did," said Oriender at exactly the same moment that O'Banion said "He did"

"There it was again," said Mike who, by concentrating hard, could just see O'Banion's outline beside the Dragon's head. O'Banion looked at Mike, then he looked at Oriender. Then he looked back at Mike

"Why don't you tell him Miko? He seems to be asking in a civilised manner."

"Why don't I tell who, and tell them what?" Miko asked in exasperation. Then he felt his tummy flutter and the world seemed to tip sideways for a moment or two. When he recovered he heard O'Banion say "Try it again now."

The voice Mike heard next was a complete surprise. It was a deep, cultured, slow voice laced with a strong sense of wisdom and patience. It was rather like Axel's voice but if Axel was at 100 on the scale of wisdom, the new voice was at 1000.

"Thank you O'Banion," The new voice said, "I haven't been able to converse with anybody for months."

"Who are you?" said Miko

"I am Oriender and I am sitting right in front of you. O'Banion has just made a few adjustments to your senses to help you communicate with me. I understand that you are Miko the Sorcerer."

Mike spluttered with surprise and disbelief. "Did you do this O'Banion?" he choked.

"Miko," said O'Banion. "Don't you know it's very rude to doubt the word of another? Oriender told you what I did, so you must believe him."

Mike turned his full attention to the dragon who was now settling down again to his lying position.

"I'm sorry," he said, "I just wasn't expecting it, even though I know O'Banion can do some very strange things. How did you find him?"

"I just called. Don't forget that Banshees leave traces of themselves everywhere they go, and if they leave someone protected, like you, the traces will be recognised anywhere in the world. That was what alerted me to your presence."

"I see," said Miko, not really seeing at all. "And what did you want to talk about?"

"Well, I was rather hoping that you would act as a means of my talking to the trolls."

"Well, strictly speaking you're not talking," interrupted O'Banion. "So Miko can't be a means of talking. But he can be a means of communication."

"Thank you O'Banion." Oriender said, with no trace of annoyance in his voice.

"You're welcome," O'Banion replied, sounding delighted with himself.

Miko was becoming slightly irritated.

"Oriender," said Miko, "I will be delighted to talk to the trolls for you. But I have no idea what to say to them. I've only just met them myself you know. I need to understand what is going on here. For instance, why are you here helping them?"

Oriender sighed a long, deep sigh.   "Ah well, there's the rub Miko. I'm not here to help them. I just fell out of the sky into this field and I believe they think I am here to help them."

"Well if you're not here for that, why are you here?"

Oriender sighed again and the flame from his nostrils turned from bright orange to deep blue. "I can see this is going to take a long time," he said. "Sit down Miko, and let me tell you a little about dragons."

Miko sat down on the ground and rested his back against the dragon's flank. It felt warm and comfortable, a feeling which was further improved when Oriender began to speak in the gentle cultured voice that Miko could hear inside his head.

Dragons are just about the oldest living things in the world Miko. We have lived here for millions of years and, apart from some arguments over food, we have not been much trouble to anybody. We live in a remote region where the mountains are high and there is little grass or trees. We build our nests in caves in the high cliffs and peaks of our homeland and we fly across the world seeking food for ourselves and our young.

"What do you eat" Miko asked.

"Birds, sheep, the occasional cow, but usually smaller animals. The trouble arises when we run into men, and more particularly dwarves, who think we eat them at any opportunity. So we try to keep ourselves to ourselves and not get in the way of trolls or the Guilds." Miko was about to interrupt with a question but the tone and timbre of Oriender's voice prevented him.

"Now dragons are highly evolved creatures who spend most of their life in the air. We launch ourselves from our nests high in the mountains and are in the air immediately. Unlike birds we can't take off from the ground by running. We dragons live for around a thousand years and we might spend seven hundred years of that flying. If an old dragon like me has to land on flat ground it usually means the end of him because he can't get back into the air and so he starves to death. Or sometimes he will be killed by men who are afraid of him. In fact such little knowledge as men have of dragons is from a number of them that landed in some swamp land thousands of years ago. I think men still call them the dragon swamps"

Miko sat listening to the dragon's sad tale. He pictured the magnificence of dragons swirling about high in the sky and the sadness of a dragon forced to land through exhaustion. His engineers mind immediately began to think of ways to overcome the problem.

"So what will you do now?" he asked Oriender.

"I can do almost nothing. I can't take off and the trolls will either kill me or try to use me. I expect they want to use me or they would have killed me already. I just wanted to have the chance to explain to them that I will die anyway if they just leave me here."

"But what if I can do something about that?" asked Miko.

"I think even you can't keep a dragon alive on the ground Miko, as powerful as you are."

"But what if I could get you back into the air. Do you have the energy to fly now?"

Yes, I could fly home now Miko. But I am more than nine hundred years old. I am stiff in my joints and my digestion is poor. The only thing I really want to do is see my great grand children again. But if that is not to be I shall die content because I have seen just about everything this world can offer."

"No you haven't. You've never seen a sorcerer like me before."

Without another word Miko stood up and made his way across the field to the entrance where Bellman and Aleric stood.

Aleric looked at Miko with a new respect in his eyes while Bellman waited for Miko to speak.

"He won't work for you and he thinks you want to kill him," said Miko, just bending the truth a little. He says he just wants to be left alone to die."

"That's no help," answered Bellman. "Half the clan leaders want him to lead the invasion of Midland. And if we try to kill him he will cause so much carnage we won't have an army left."

"I think I could arrange for him to leave," said Mike, "but it would take some extra special sorcery."

"Could you? Could you do that for us Miko? It would help me a lot of you could."

"Let me have a look round and then talk to the dragon once more," said Mike. "Then I'll tell you whether I can do it."

Mike walked around the field and examined the slope down the hill from every angle. He measured some angles and the height of some of the trees and generally mystified Bellman and Aleric. When he had finished he went back and had a further long conversation with Oriender.

After that he went to the Rover and took out some paper and pencils and set about drawing. As he worked Bellman and Aleric looked over his shoulder but neither was able to make anything of the sketches Mike produced.

All the time he worked Mike was aware of O'Banion in the background asking questions.

"How will this work Miko? What do you need that for? What if this event happens or if that event doesn't happen." Mike dealt with the Banshee as best he could while continuing to work. He knew it was no good asking him to leave or telling him to shut up, so he just kept on working and tried to answer the O'Banion's questions without letting it interrupt his work. By the early afternoon he had finished.

He showed the drawing to Bellman. "This spell will help the dragon to leave Southend and avoid him laying waste to your army. I can do this if you can get the agreement of the other clan leaders to allow a group of trolls to work under my supervision."

Bellman muttered to himself about the problems of management but eventually declared that he thought he could fix it if the dragon could just do a little more to suggest that he really would destroy Southend given the chance.

Mike went back for another conversation with Oriender and the dragon stood up again. With a lot of care, none of which was obvious to the watching Trolls, Oriender walked to the edge of the field and looked at the fence. Then with a mild shake of his head, which filled the trolls with dread, he butted the fence down and stepped outside the field. He selected a direction and began to blow down the hill. At first nothing was very visible, but soon the smoke which came from his nostrils turned into pale blue flame and then into bright, incandescent orange which struck the pine trees and burned down everything in its path.

Aleric and Bellman watched in fear as Mike walked around the dragon egging him on with words of encouragement. By the time the dragon had finished there was a clear path straight down the steepest side of the hill for several hundred yards. Mike smiled to himself and walked back to Bellman.

"Now," he said, "If you can do your bit we can begin. And by the time I am finished everybody will know the name of Miko the Sorcerer.

A New Broom

Mike stood with Bellman examining the latest handiwork of the trolls. He was impressed. In the seven days since he had arrived in Southend the trolls, working to his directions, had achieved miracles

Firstly Bellman had gathered the other clan leaders together and taken them to the hilltop where Oriender lay waiting. The devastation around the field was enough to convince most of them that he was not about to help them with the Guilds and he was ready to lay waste the whole of Southend if riled.

Mike had taken a team of Trolls and begun his project immediately. The clearing of the path burned out by the dragon and the collection of a lot of high quality lumber were first on the list. By following Mike's instructions closely the trolls had built a set of legs which were set in the soil of the side of the hill and used these to support a platform which ran level from the top of the hill for about ten feet. They had then built a longer pair of legs and used this to support the platform for a further ten feet. By repeating this process over and over again they had extended the platform until it ran for more than one hundred feet from the top of the hill. Mike had then covered the platform in strong timber boards and walked out along the platform until he was standing some twenty-five feet above the ground over the timber clad side of the hill.

He had then walked back to Oriender and spent some fifteen minutes in conversation with him   During the conversation Oriender stood up to his full height, an action which terrified the trolls working on the platform, and had spread his wings to their full span. Mike marveled at the engineering of Oriender's wings. They were fifty feet each and changed from strong muscular construction at the front and close to his body, to fine almost feathery structure at the ends.

Mike had asked Oriender about the techniques of flying and could now clearly see why the dragon could not take off. His wingspan was so great that when he flapped his wings downward they hit the floor. Mike judged that the dragon would need to be almost forty feet above ground to take off. Grimly he returned to the platform.

He walked out along the platform once more, checking the strength and firmness of the walkway. It seemed okay but he would not be sure until he could test it properly.

Taking his time Mike returned to his drawings and made some adjustments. Then he called the trolls together and explained what he wanted. Oriender just watched and waited as Mike set the trolls to work and then climbed into his magical transporter and left the site.

After his conversations with Oriender, Mike had thought his way round the rest of his situation. Since Esmeralda had left in a huff he had a fair idea that the Guilds would have given up on him. Thinking of the character of the people in Midland he decided that only three of them would have any idea of what to do. By putting himself in their shoes he decided that his first priority would have to be the defence of Southend if a bloodbath were to be avoided. He had talked to Bellman and told the troll of the conclusions he had reached. Then, with the help of some troll builders he had designed a defence barrier for the troll gate.

The trolls, under Mike's supervision, had erected a barrier across the troll gate that would keep out the most unwelcome callers. It had taken a lot of organising. There had been two days to design it and four days of furious activity to complete it. It comprised a wooden barrier which ran from one side of the pass to the other at a point chosen for the narrowness of the path and the steepness of its sides The dwarves would have to go over it or through it. Mike doubted their ability to do either.

As an additional precaution, however, he had set up a rockslide which could be triggered to block the pass completely if necessary. He was very pleased indeed with his handiwork.

He had also used the time to frame the questions he wanted to answer about the relationship between Midland and Southend. Seven days of thinking had given him a solution. He had tried bits of it at the Monolith library and other bits of it with Bellman. The rest of the council had refused to speak to him as they did not really believe his assertions of innocence in the case of eating babies and thought he did a good job of hiding his fangs.

As he stood at the barricade he decided that the time had come to open the play on the on the third part of the solution.

"This should delay the Guilds for some time Bellman. What do you think?" "It certainly should. If they attack as you say they will. I just hope we can get rid of the Dragon before they do. The last thing I want is the Guilds fighting us this side and a Dragon chewing into our forces from the rear"

"Don't worry" said Mike. "They'll attack alright. And I'll take care of the Dragon very soon"

"Then we should be able to delay the Guilds. I'm not sure what good that will do us. It seems to me that it only makes it more difficult for us to undertake the journey. We can't fly over them and we certainly can't go through them. That doesn't leave much else that's practical, or even feasible."

"That remains to be seen Bellman. How many trolls do you think it will take to keep this pass adequately defended?"

"No more than two thousand could do the job. Three thousand if you want to minimise fatigue and give them regular changes. They should be able to hold this place forever."

"That's what I thought. That leaves you with a lot of able-bodied trolls. Trolls to apply to the problem of completing the journey. If things work out the way I hope then we have the two things we need, time and muscle." Mike had a faraway look in his eye when he spoke. He was brought back to reality with a thump when Bellman said,

"The Guilds must be approaching. The trolls we sent out as lookouts are all coming back." Mike looked and saw about fifty trolls making their way at speed to the troll gate. Ropes were lowered over the barrier and the trolls climbed them with their usual speed and agility which never ceased to amaze Mike. One of them approached Bellman and the sorcerer.

"Dwarves," he said. "Thousands of them. Approaching from all directions. This could be the biggest fight in history."

"But it won't," said Bellman quickly, "because we are only going to hold them here. Your task will be to keep the Guilds at bay for at least a month. You should be able to do that without ever getting into a fight. If we have to, we can block the pass permanently but there should be no need for that. For now Miko and I will have to leave to organize other things but keep me informed if anything happens."

As Mike and Bellman left the trolls were preparing for a siege. They were walking back to the Rover when O'Banion suddenly materialised beside Mike. Mike could not see the Banshee but he knew he was there.

"I wish you wouldn't do that." Mike snapped in irritation.

"Do what?" asked Bellman, puzzled by Mike's outburst.

"Sorry Bellman, nothing for you to worry about."

After that Mike began to think loudly at the Banshee, a trick he had learned at the dragon pen. "Why are you here?" Mike thought,

"Why are any of us here Miko? It's the really big question isn't it? And as nice as it would be to spend time debating it with a man of your intellect, I don't have time right now. I've come to tell you that Oriender thinks the Trolls have finished your spell. He thought you would want to know.

"Okay," Mike thought in reply, "Go back and tell Oriender to get as much rest as he can. I'll be with you tomorrow morning." The turning to Bellman he said "We have to go back to the Dragon pen. I think it's time to finalise the spell to get rid of the dragon."

Bellman looked at Mike with awe. The sorcerer seemed to be able to divine messages out of the air.

The next morning at first light Mike and Bellman were at the field where Oriender was dozing lightly. Mike walked out to the platform built by the trolls and began to inspect it in detail. He climbed up and down the sides of it and jumped up and down on the platform itself. At one stage he had twenty troll jumping up and down in time at the end of the platform which now stood almost fifty feet above the ground. Mike watched the structure carefully as the trolls jumped in time. He tested joints and felt the vibration which ran through the woodwork. After two hours of testing he felt ready for the real test.

He stood beside Oriender and called gently to the sleepy dragon.

"Oriender, it's time for you to show us what you're made of.

The great Dragon opened first one eye and then the other. "Are you sure this is the right thing to do Miko. I could just lie here and fade away. It would be quite painless you know."

"Not for us it wouldn't," the sorcerer replied. "We need you to survive. More than that we need you to send a message."

"Okay Miko, You win. I went along with your ideas so far because I thought it would never work. But now I see that you are a greater sorcerer than these people realise. Let us get on with it."

Oriender stood up and began to plod laboriously across the field. Each footstep sent a slight tremor through the ground and Mike began to worry about the strength of his platform. As the dragon approached it the trolls, under Bellman's command, withdrew to the other side of the field.

"Now," said Mike, as Oriender approached the platform. "Small steps please, just as we discussed."

"What do you mean by small?" chipped in O'Banion. "A small step for a dragon is a huge step for mankind. Do you mean small for him or small for you?"

"He knows what I mean," said Mike through gritted teeth. "So just let's be quiet and let him get on with it."

Oriender walked, timidly at first, out onto the beginning of the platform. The boards bent a little under his weight but they held firm as he made his initial slow progress out over the hillside. The whole structure began to shiver slightly as the dragon increased his stride. Mike spoke soothingly and gently all the time as Oriender walked out along the platform. He also kept a sharp eye on the support structure, looking for weak joints or bending support struts.

Oriender continued placing one foot in front of the other until he was half way along the platform, then he stopped.

"What's the matter Oriender?" Mike asked.

"Nothing at all," replied the dragon's soothing tones. I just need to concentrate on my balance, so I am going to open my wings."

Standing in the middle of the platform the dragon opened his wings to their full span and Mike was, once again, reminded of what magnificent creatures these dragons were. Iridescent colour ran the length of the wings and the light seemed to be reflected at all angles.

"Having my wings open helps me to balance," the dragon said as he began to move the wings gently up and down. "And if there is any wind it will take some of my weight."

Mike, Bellman and a group of awestruck trolls held their breath and watched as Oriender continued his journey along the platform. There was perfect silence broken only by the creaking of the structure as it moved and flexed beneath the weigh of the mighty creature. The time between steps increased and the movement in the structure became greater with each step Oriender took.

With just ten feet left to go the dragon stretched his wings downward and found they were clear of the ground. The motion of his wings lifted him slightly and when his weight settled back onto the wooden structure there was a slight wrenching sound as two of the timbers in the structure on one side were torn by the stress of the dragon's movement. The platform tilted very slightly. Not enough to be seen by a casual observer but certainly enough for Oriender's sophisticated sense of balance to detect. Mike also saw it and began to speak to the dragon more quickly.

"Now is the time Oriender. You have to go to the end of the platform and launch yourself off. It's starting to bend under your weight. It will support you for while but as soon as you can you need to get into the air. Please go."

Bellman and the trolls had all overcome their fears and crossed the field where they now stood beside Mike watching as the dragon took two more large steps and reached the end of the platform. There was a terrible tearing sound as timbers began to split and splinter apart. The weight of the dragon pushed the platform to one side as some of the timber below buckled and broke. Mike held his breath as he saw Oriender begin to move down on the slowly collapsing platform. Then with a mighty movement of his wings the dragon lifted his feet from the platform and launched off into the air. The sound of his wings was deafening as he fought to gain altitude. The colours in his wings sparkled and spangled in the sunlight as he felt control coming back to him and began to soar up into the air.

In spite of their fear the troll broke into spontaneous cheering as the dragon lifted higher and higher into the air leaving the platform a collapsing pile of matchwood in the ground.

"Miko, that was splendid," O'Banion said into Mike's ear. "I'm delighted to have been here to see it and I'm sure it will go down in dragon history as well as the troll legends. But I'm afraid I can't stay here any longer to help you. I have to get back to Gloom Wood. If you need any more help with your sorcery, just call me."

Mike thought he would and then thought goodbye at the Banshee who just faded from Mike's conscious as though he had never been there.

Turning his attention back to the sky Mike watched Oriender travelling in circles and soaring higher and higher into the sky until he could no longer be seen. Then he turned to Bellman and said, with a slight quiver in his voice. "That's that done. I hope he remembers to do what we asked him."

"Well Miko, if I had any doubts about you they were just washed away entirely. That was stunning. Not just the bold conception of the spell, but the execution of it in such a short space of time.   And that last part, making it self-destruct just as the dragon lifted off, so that other people couldn't copy it. That was masterful."

Mike was about to reply when he heard Oriender's voice in his head. "Miko, how can I ever thank you? I never thought I would see the world again from up here, but I have thanks to you, and it's just as wonderful as it always was."

"Just remember to do what I asked on you way home pal. And have a good flight."

Turning to Bellman Mike said "Let's get back to Monolith. We still have a lot to do."

The two companions reached Monolith after a completely silent journey and went straight to Bellman's private library. The troll ordered drinks to be brought in and then turned to face Mike.

"Well Miko, now we are committed to your plans, so I hope the rest are as good as what I've seen so far."

"Oh they are Bellman. They are. I am going to invent a completely new spell just for the trolls. It will take a little time for your trolls to master the spell but I'm sure they will manage in the long run. Do you have a map of the whole country?"

Bellman produced a map and laid it on the table. Mike stood over it for a moment and then pointed,

"What's this Bellman?"

"It's the sea."

"How were the edges charted?"

"By broom. How else would you do it?"

"How else indeed Bellman? Well I'm going to show you how else and at the same time I will show you a way to get from the bottom of this land to the top without going over the Guild's territory."

"You mean without a broom?"

"Yes I'll show you a ship. That's a spell which can be put together without moonbeams or starlight, doesn't need rhinoceros horn or newts tails or sunbeams or any of the things that you can't afford for brooms. All you need is timber, muscle and love."

"What is a ship? Is it some sort of alternative to a broom?"

"Yes Bellman." Mike laughed. "That's exactly what it is. It's a new broom, which is going to sweep warfare from the land. It's a spell that I shall cast on the water and once it's been cast you can use it to transport large groups of people around the edge of the land without ever going over it. Your people will go round the edge of the land to the top of the country, and then you can do what you like." He showed Bellman the possibility of travelling over the sea but the troll could not grasp the idea at all.

"Don't worry," said Mike, "I'll show you what I mean. All I want is a thousand trolls and one month. In that time I can cast for you such a spell as has never been seen in this land,"

The fire in Mike's eyes filled Bellman with a delightful mixture of apprehension and excitement. He knew he would give Mike the resources he wanted but worried about leaving so much of importance to the schemes of a mad, wild-eyed sorcerer even though he knew what Miko could do.

If Mike's work with Oriender had been exhausting his activity with the trolls was more so. Sorcerer and trolls worked all the hours of daylight available and then some. Mike found the trolls to be capable workers with a thirst for new knowledge and minds quick enough to grasp it. His major problem was that of design. Having decided to show the trolls how to build a boat he had very little other knowledge to fall back on. Beside his knowledge of engineering and a general idea of what a boat should look like he was working in the dark. The trolls, however, proved to be particularly inventive once they were given the basic idea on which the spell for ships operated.

Over the course of the three weeks following the first attack by the Guilds Mike had produced a number of sketches of rudimentary vessels and two small working models. The trolls had picked up the idea quickly and by working in teams on both design and construction they had produced a very creditable small boat. It was about twenty-five yards long with a single mast and a geared tiller.

The problem was that it had been built on a beach and there was no way of getting it to the water. This tended to reduce the troll's faith in Mike's sorcering abilities but his solution had re-established it more firmly than ever. Instead of trying to take the boat to the sea he had brought the sea to the boat by digging a channel from the water line to the sand on which the boat sat. As the water came nearer to the boat the sodden sand began to slip from under the boat into the channel, It had taken a lot of trolls to steady the boat and a lot more to dig the channel but eventually the boat had slipped somewhat uneasily into the sea.

Bellman was among the first of the trolls to board the ship and had spent a great deal of time inspecting it for leaks, then worrying about how small it was. With a million trolls to transport it would take a great many such ships to complete the journey. The trolls could produce some but surely not enough to complete the journey. This did not worry Mike. He was more concerned that Bellman and the rest of the council accept the principle of sea travel.

"You see Bellman," he told the troll as they walked around the ship for the third time, "These vessels can carry a great amount freight as well as men. Once you have mastery of the sea you can go anywhere you wish."

"But Miko, we don't wish to go 'anywhere'. We only want to go to the troll country."

"That may be true for now but what of the future?"

"The future can take care of itself Miko. We've never got as far as this before. With your magic we can definitely make enough ships for the journey, provided we are prepared to wait."

"And there you have it Bellman. Are you prepared to wait? You have the physical resources but will your people rest easy for the length of time involved, particularly as they don't really know how long it will be.

"What choice do we have Miko? We have the means and we have the time. We must use them as best we can."

"I suppose you must," said Mike and then changing the subject with the deftness of a berserk blacksmith he said, "How is the defence against the Guilds going Bellman?"

"Well we're keeping them out, but in the end, if they remain as persistent as they have been over the past three weeks, I can see no alternative but all out war with them."

"And then what happens to the ships and the journey?"

"I don't know Miko. To be honest, when you first brought up the subject of the spell for ships I had no idea it would be so complicated. I rather hoped that we would be much further down the road than we are now. Oh not that I intend to belittle your efforts Miko. You are indeed the greatest sorcerer of all time and we are very lucky that you didn't just confine your efforts to the side of the Guilds. it's just that ..well I feel now that to meet the task allotted to you would take powers even beyond yours, and such power is not easily available. Consequently, as I said before, we must use what we have available. We will try to keep the Guilds at bay and build ships. But if we have to fight, then we have to."

Mike shook his head in wonder at the mixture of fatalism and optimism displayed by Bellman. It seemed typical of troll philosophy.

"I think I can do something else for you Bellman, but I need a lot of help, probably from your council. Now that I've demonstrated my good faith, could you fix it for me to talk to them?"

Bellman was uncertain about that. He fretted and paced up and down the ship for fifteen or more minutes before he finally agreed to try. Three days later Mike addressed the Southend Planning Authority.

He had, in fact, taken a full four weeks preparing for this address. It had been one of a series of major milestones in his plan. Like all the others it was critical, but unlike many of them be had only one shot. If he did not convince them the first time he would not get another chance. In the middle of the afternoon he faced the assembled clan lenders. He spoke with a confidence he did not feel.

"Gentlemen," he began, "Or perhaps I should say gentle trolls, for it has been my experience that trolls are much more gentle than men, or dwarves, would ever be. I am Miko the sorcerer. I am, as you can see, without fangs and I have lived on troll food very comfortably for five or six weeks now. I have banished a dragon, built a barrier against the Guilds, also I have given you a spell which will enable you to make the journey you wish, provided that you have time to cast it properly. It is about that aspect of the problem that I would like to speak now." The trolls shuffled their feet and cleared their throats while Mike let his opening remarks sink in.

"I now come before you to say that if you are not careful you will not have that time. The Guilds are literally knocking at the door. Pretty soon they will knock the door down." This reminder of the nearness of the Guilds unsettled the audience for a moment. Mike let them murmur for a few seconds and then continued. "I, however, can do something to prevent this from happening."

Landsman, who was somewhat bolder than most of his fellow councilors, spoke up. "What is it you think you can do that good trolls can't?"

"I think I can get the Guilds to let you alone. But I would require your total co-operation."

"Why should we trust you?" put in Fireman.

"Why shouldn't we? He banished the dragon and gave us the ship spell," responded Dustman, before Mike could answer.

The debate over the trustworthiness of sorcerers in general and Miko in particular, continued for some minutes. Eventually Bellman intervened. He banged the table with his gavel.

"My friends.. please. Perhaps before we go any further it would be a good idea to find out how this trust and co-operation would manifest itself." There was a murmur of agreement followed by a silence. Mike took advantage of it to start again.

"If you are to be free of the Guilds you must convince them that it is in their interest to stop harassing you. If you would be prepared to follow my instructions I think I can convince them of that."

The conversation continued for some hours. By the time it had finished Mike was hoarse and thirsty. The council had agreed to test his ideas out between themselves and come back to him the next day. After he had left they took a vote on his proposal and accepted it, just,

The following day he explained his plan to them in detail.

The Guild's Solution

Axel gave Esmeralda another glass of mulled winter ale. It was her third. Her face was tearstained and her appearance disheveled. Axel looked serious and puzzled. The only other person in the room was Bandor who kept pacing around the room and muttering to himself. The three of them were in Axel's apartment.

Having returned from Monolith to the bridge Esmeralda had found the other two but had been incoherent. They had brought her back to the university and given her a stiff drink. After a little bullying she had told them roughly what had happened in Monolith.

"And you're sure," said Axel, "That Miko's plan had nothing in it about wiping out the trolls."

"Yes I'm sure. We questioned him very closely about that. Ask Wilberforce. He was there."

"We will, as soon as he comes out of shock. Now tell me again what Miko said."

"He said he had made a deal with the trolls to let them run all over Midland."

"Did he actually use those words? -run all over Midland- or was it just a similar phrase."

"Oh I don't know. Let me think. I can't remember properly. He said he'd made a deal which allowed the trolls to do what they liked... No that wasn't it... It was to do as they wanted...No it wasn't that either., Oh yes. They could go where they wanted, that was it. The trolls could go where they wanted to."

"And it wasn't any sort of code. He wasn't trying to disguise his meaning for the benefit of any others present."

"There were no others present. Just Miko, Wilberforce and me."

"But Axel," Bandor suddenly interrupted. "He knows that we won't let the trolls into Midland without a fight. Therefore he must mean to wipe us out. If that's the case we will have to do something about it first." As he spoke the dwarf continued to pace around the room.

"Well I do not believe that Miko would be party to wiping us out," said Axel, "But just in case the trolls do have that in mind what do you think we should do Bandor?"

"We could beat them to it. Send some of our best dwarves into Southend to obliterate them before they have the chance to burst out and over-run Midland."

"That's easier said than done. What about the trolls already here. They are destroying our food supplies."

"Well they can't destroy them all and if we can get beyond the troll gate we will have access to their supplies,

"What about the dragons?" asked Esmeralda suddenly taking interest in the conversation.

"The crossbows that Miko magicked up for us can keep the dragons at bay." The mention of Miko's name sent Esmeralda off into floods of tears once again.

"Alright Bandor," said Axel. "How long will it take to get our forces ready to invade Southend and finish the trolls?"

"We shall have to collect them into larger groups and explain the situation to them. We need more weapons to replace those lost in the skirmishes. Then we'll have to get them worked up for a major rumble. I should say we could be ready in six days.. maybe seven.

"Good. In that case we had better get Leander working on collecting the supplies into fewer depots."

It was agreed that Axel would organize the supplies with Leander and Bandor would fix up the fighting forces. The rest of the people who had been working in Miko's organization were either too upset, like Esmeralda and Wilberforce, to be of any use, or they just would not work for Bandor or Axel. Consequently the dwarf and the wizard spent the next six days in a frenzy of activity such as had not been seen around the University in years.

On the evening of the sixth day they sat again in Axel's apartment discussing progress. Bandor held forth for some ten minutes on the state of readiness of the dwarfish fighting force. They were, it seemed, in prime condition. Axel however was concerned about other things. He wore a worried frown as he explained them to Bandor.

"You see Bandor, it's all very well having the troops in good shape and spoiling for a fight but do we have the backup services that we need'? The number of good wizards that we can put into the field to help your mammoth fighting force is limited to Esmeralda, myself and a lot of eager but inexperienced students. Normally that might be okay but this time we are taking on something bigger than we have ever considered before. In the past we could get by with a couple of us running round assisting with the odd bolt of lightning here and a small rockslide there. This time we are putting all our dwarves in one basket as it were, and I don't know if we have the right resources. Particularly as Esmeralda is so upset by the whole business. I'm afraid that you will end up being supported by a lot of willing students who don't have the experience to be effective."

"Well I'm not too worried about the level of support we get. At the minute the dwarves would hang by their toes from the ceiling if we asked them to. On the other hand I don't want to waste good people if it can be avoided so, the more help we can get from your wizards, the better I shall like it. We should certainly ask Esmeralda to help. I haven't seen her for a couple of days and she may have used the time to pull herself together."

Axel considered this for a moment and realised that he too had not seen the witch for the past two days. It might, he thought, be worth getting her into the discussion. They were just about to look for her when she appeared at the door. Her demeanor had improved immensely since either of them had last seen her. She was calm and in control of herself .

"Ah" she said, "I heard you were both here so I thought I'd better come along and find out what is happening. When do we begin the assault on Southend?"

"Now that you are here we can discuss just that Esmeralda. Bandor says the troops are ready and it will be bad for them if we delay any longer. It really depends on whether you feel up to controlling a contingent of Wizardry. We don't have anyone else of the required calibre."

"In that case we have no problems, we can march against the trolls tomorrow. Don't worry about me. I've been doing some serious thinking and I have decided that I can't let Miko's defection stand between me and the safety of the Guilds."

This was followed by a deepening silence so Axel decided to close the meeting before the subject of Miko became the central theme. "Okay, we'll start the troops out first thing in the morning. In the meantime we'd all do well to catch up on some sleep."

After he had ushered the other two out the tall wizard folded his frame into his favourite chair and went over the happenings of the last month in his mind. He could not understand where things had gone wrong. He was not even certain that they had gone wrong. He tapped the table beside him twice and a small glass of wine appeared beside him, He lifted it to his lips but was disturbed by the voice of his wife.

"Its no wonder we can't keep any wine in this house. You keep on drinking it,"

"Yes dear. Why don't you come and sit down and tell me what you think about the war so far?"

"Oh you and your blastworthy war, I suppose you have to go. You always do. I'll tell you one thing though, be very careful about Esmeralda. There's something worrying that girl. She's under a lot of strain and likely to crack. I think she's been taking her granny's potions to help her out."

"Good grief, I do hope not. If her granny were alive today she'd never get a license for those potions of hers, except perhaps the love potion. Most of them were lethal."

"Well, lethal or not, she's taking them so be careful with her when you get to the fighting."

After Morag had left Axel sat and thought some more about the impending fight. His heart was not really in it but he could see no other alternative open to him. He finished his wine with one long swallow and rose from the chair. A night's sleep, he told himself, would make everything that much clearer. Tomorrow would be time enough for worrying.

A Change of Heart

Bandor was furious. For the best part of a month the cream of the dwarf's fighting forces had been pitted against the barrier across the troll gate and in that time they had made no impression whatever. Axel and Esmeralda had used their powers to the limit. They had hurled fire, water and rocks against the barrier but in all cases the sorcery of Miko and the trolls had proved too much for them. Their small army of wizards had retired, thoroughly worn out and dispirited, after a month of trying everything they knew, all to no avail.

The situation had been made worse by the occasional arrival of a dragon, the biggest that Bandor had ever seen, who would fly above the dwarves' camp, just out of range of the cross bows, breathing fire and spreading fear among even the most experienced troops.

Bandor's humour had become worse and worse. The trolls succeeded in making the dwarves look foolish and ineffectual. Admittedly losses had been minimal. A few dwarves had been burned by Axel's lightning bolts and one had suffered a fractured skull from a rock which had bounced off the barrier when Esmeralda threw it, along with several very large boulders. But that was no reason to feel pleased.

"I wish now we'd never heard of this stupid idea to hire a sorcerer," he said as he walked up and down in the tent that served as their field headquarters. "So far all we've done is squander a lot of good wizardry for nothing. We've run out of arrows for the crossbows without killing one dragon that we know of. And all our brooms are so badly run down that we can't charge them up in the field. Most of them will have to go back to General Brooms for an overhaul. That's going to cost us a fortune."

"Alright Bandor," Axel interrupted, "we know things aren't going too well but getting more het up wont do anything to relieve the situation. We have to think positively about what to do. There is, after all, a positive side to this situation."

"I know, I know. Losses are down to nothing. We've never lost so few in a fight with the trolls. But this is no fight for a dwarf."

"I was thinking more of the fact that Miko, by going over to the other side, may have done us a favour. He may even have succeeded in doing what we hired him for."

"What do you mean?"

"Well, while I admit that we can't get into Southend to attack the trolls, they cannot get out. This is as much a barrier for them as it is for us. A small contingent of dwarves camped here could guard this pass against the total might of the troll forces."

"That's no good to me. We dwarf warriors want to fight, not guard. In the old days it was fine. A good rumble with the trolls every so often gets the aggression out of our system. Guarding a pass doesn't do that."

"No. I can see that. But I can't offer you much other consolation. We've tried everything science can offer to remove the barrier. Pyrotechnics, Levitation, Telekinesis.

None of it works. Some of the students at the university have even turned their hands to elementary sorcery in an effort to help but nothing seems to work against Miko's power."

"Miko, Miko, Miko. All I hear is Miko. There has to be a way around that barrier, or over it, through it or even under it. There has to be."

"Why?" asked Esmeralda. "If nothing else, Miko was a powerful sorcerer. There is no reason at all why we should be able to overcome his barrier."

"Well we'll just stay here until the barrier falls down or we find some other way. Dwarves don't give up that easily."

"Nobody mentioned giving up, Bandor, but we must face facts. Keeping this army here is doing nothing for the economy. It's just eating up food pointlessly. Why don't we withdraw all but a token force until we find a way of beating the trolls? And then we can reassemble the army."

"If we let them go now we'll never get them back again at short notice. You can't fight a war with most of the army on leave."

In fact the trio had been over this argument many times before. Bandor always ended by refusing to withdraw his troops and they would obey nobody else. Axel and Esmeralda always lost their tempers with Bandor's attitude and ended by returning to the University for a day. The atmosphere in the tent was getting acrimonious when Wilberforce burst in.

"Something's happening at the barrier. I think you should come and look."

Four weeks of campaign experience had done a great deal to harden the goblin's nerves. All four of them left the tent and went to the centre of the pass from where they could get a good view of the barrier. As they watched the centre of the offending structure moved slightly. Bandor fidgeted, debating whether to alert the dwarves for a sudden attack if the opportunity presented itself.

The centre of the barrier was slowly being removed. Axel restrained Bandor from issuing any orders and everybody watched, fearing the worst. Wilberforce was sure that the world's biggest dragon was about to be released. None of the others formed an opinion. When the central section was completely gone the whole of the dwarf contingent waited with bated breath for what would be the first aggressive move by the trolls since the barrier had appeared. As they watched, out into the afternoon sunlight came Miko, sitting alone on his transporter.

Had he but realised how close he would come to sudden death Mike would have thought twice about coming out of the barrier. He was met by a massive silence, closely followed by a bevy of axes and clubs, thrown by anybody within reach, a tirade of dwarfish abuse, thrown by Bandor, a bolt of lightning thrown by Esmeralda and Axel's staff. Either by luck, or by virtue of Axel's extraordinary skills, the first thing to reach Mike was the wizard's staff.

As the leading end of the staff made contact the Rover, with its contents, was lifted high into the air and disappeared from sight. Bandor turned to Axel and snarled, "What have you done with him? Bring him back so that I can kill him. At least let me break one of his legs or a couple of ribs."

"Bandor, has it occurred to you that Miko may be returning to us for a reason? You have already been guilty of misjudging him once, don't let's make the same mistake again, If Miko has no explanation which is acceptable then you can both maim and kill him at the same time as far as I'm concerned."

The dwarf accepted Axel's comments with mumbled disapproval. Esmeralda sat in strained silence. She had great difficulty in preventing a sudden flow of tears. Axel continued, "It seems to me that Miko must have something to tell us or he would never have come out of that barrier alone. He's been gone from us for a period of five weeks or so during which time we have had minimal losses and the trolls have not been seen in Midland. I think we should listen very closely to anything he has to say before we commit ourselves to actions which will seem foolish later."

Everybody seemed to accept Axel's council without further argument but there was little enthusiasm for the idea. Axel continued again.

"If we must do this we may as well do it in the comfort of the University. Bandor, I'm sure the dwarves can stop worrying now. There won't be any fighting. If we can all meet in my apartment in one hour I promise to have Miko ready for questioning."

When Axel had finished Bandor just shook his head and walked off to organise the return of some of the dwarves. Esmeralda immediately returned to the University to change her clothes and repair her face. Wilber looked worried and went straight to the University bar. Axel collected a few things together and delayed until everybody else had left then he snapped his fingers and his staff appeared in his hand. This was closely followed by Mike, who had been sitting in the Rover and suddenly found himself sitting on fresh air. He fell to the ground with a thump.

"What on earth is all this?" he demanded of Axel. "I do a great job for you, I come back expecting you to be pleased and what happens? I get cursed, shouted at, have axes and lightning thrown at me and finally I get taken off to who knows where. What's it all about Axel?"

"Miko, I expect you to have an explanation, but please don't expect me to believe that you have not been helping the trolls for the last month. That barrier is obviously your work as were the preparations for our assault on it."

Mike smiled at the tall wizard. Then he said, "Well there's no need to worry now because I've done the job you wanted. I'll explain it all when we get back to the university."

"You certainly will Miko. But I should warn you that I am making some conditions concerning your explanation. First, if it is not satisfactory you will be tried by the Guild court for unauthorised passing of secrets. Second, even if it is, both Bandor and Esmeralda are after your blood for making them look silly."

"Well," said Mike, smiling with a confidence he did not feel, "In that case I'll have to make sure my explanation is better than just good."

"Yes. You had. You are due to be questioned at my apartment in some forty minutes time."

"Excellent. But I must insist on one thing. I want the whole of the negotiating committee there. I don't want to have to go through the whole deal twice or three times as extra people come in."

"You, Miko, are in no position to insist on anything. But I suppose you're right

"Good," said Mike. "I'm looking forward to hearing your reactions and, I might add, your apologies. I think I might even ask for a bonus."

Two hours later Mike stood before the whole of the negotiating committee. It had taken Axel all of the intervening time to collect the group together and Mike had refused to say a word until they were all gathered. When Axel eventually presented him to the group he was greeted by a stony silence. He checked the critical members of the group for his plan. He did not need them all by any means but the insistence on their presence added dramatic impact to his performance. He coughed lightly to clear his throat and began to speak,

"Where shall I begin?" he said looking directly at Esmeralda. "It seems to me that you people brought me here and made a bargain. In return for a certain amount of gold I was to assist you in removing the menace of the trolls. Well, now I can tell you that I have done it. The trolls will never be seen again in Midland. In fact, by the end of the next ten days there won't be a troll left in Southend. They will be gone forever." This statement brought gasps from everyone. Bandor was the first to react.

"What about that barrier you built to prevent us from attacking the trolls eh? You can't deny that, can you? Why didn't you let us in to murder a few of them? And what about the deal you made with the troll leaders allowing them to go where they wanted to. Esmeralda told us all about that."

"Look Bandor, I'm a sorcerer, not a self defence instructor. I need peace and quiet to work my spells in. How can I be expected to work when I'm being attacked by either trolls or dwarves. As for the deal I made with Bellman, how else was I to get the time to do any real sorcering? I had to come up with something really special to get rid of all those trolls. It's not the sort of thing that can be done in five minutes."

"Well why did you not tell me about it when I was there?" asked
Esmeralda.

"I tried to at first, but you wouldn't listen. You kept asking me if I was going to wipe them out. How could I answer you and keep the trolls happy enough to let me work on them for a month. Anyway, it was better that you went off in a huff, It gave the whole thing an air of authenticity."

"Just stop there Miko. " said Axel. "We've had enough of the problems. Let's hear about the solutions. What have you done with the trolls to stop them invading Midland and make them leave Southend?"

"I told them I'd give them a spell that would let them go where they wanted to."

"There. I told you so." Esmeralda almost shouted.

"And then I made up a spell which would do two things. First give them the ability to leave Southend without going through Midland and second make them want to go far away from Midland. In fact as far as possible."

At this the general interest around the table began to increase.

"To go where Miko?" Axel asked.

"To the lands beyond the sea."

"But Miko, travel to the lands beyond the sea is incredibly expensive and too far for kinetic travel. The Guilds have sent out expeditions before now to meet the people from these other lands, but it's not an economic proposition. The cost of charging a broom up enough to cover the distance both ways to the nearest other country is astonishing. How will the trolls be able to pay for all this?"

"They won't have to. I've given them a spell that lets them do it for nothing."

Lutetia almost choked when Mike said this.

"You've done what?" she gasped. "You've given them a spell which lets them go to other places for nothing. You've given them the secret of free broom travel which we've been searching for since forever, investing at ludicrously high levels, keeping faerie scientists going on nothing else without ever getting a penny back from it. And you've given it to the trolls."

When she stopped for a moment Mike did not know whether she was speechless or just winding up for another tirade. He decided it was the latter and smiled to himself as he prepared to bait her further,

"Well it's not really broom travel at all, although I told the trolls it was a sort of new broom." Lutetia relaxed. "It's a totally new type of transport." Lutetia began to explode again, very slowly. "But don't worry. It need not interfere with your research, I've built it into the spell that the trolls can't give the secret to anybody else. They can give them a working model of course, but they can't pass on the secret of the way it works."

There was a general babble which was overcome by Lutetia screaming.

"That's even worse. The trolls have done nothing to earn this secret and they can't give it to us. All they can do is sell the working effect to everyone in the world and make a fortune. That's all they can do." Mike put on his most ingenuous face and had trouble in not laughing.

"But Lutetia, I thought you wanted to be allowed to complete your research, I have ensured that you can and that when you do the trolls can't interfere with your market.

"What market? There won't be a market by then you dummy. The trolls will have destroyed it with your alternative transport."

Mike looked glum.

"I hadn't thought of that. But there's not much I can do now. The trolls will all be gone in ten days and it would take me months to dismantle the spell and reconstruct it some other way."

Axel decided that it was time to get the meeting under control again.

"Everybody please, can we wait a moment. This issue is going to take some thought. It's fair to say that Miko has explained his behaviour with the trolls, unless anyone wants to go into that again, so I suggest we adjourn for an hour. Let's collect our thoughts on what Miko has just told us and reconvene in an hour. Then we can ask Miko some questions which mean something to him and to us. I, in the meantime, will explain the problem to Miko in terms that even a child could understand. It seems that sorcerers are even simpler than we thought."

As soon as Axel had finished speaking the room virtually emptied. Mike was left with the tall wizard. He was rather disappointed to find that Esmeralda had not stayed, or at least spoken to him. Axel interrupted his thoughts by saying

"Come over here and sit down Miko. It seems that I have to give you a lesson in simple economics," Mike sat down and tried to look puzzled. It was still difficult to avoid laughing.

"It's like this Miko," Axel began, "We have a simple rural economy in this country. We don't have an internal supply of stardust or moonbeams so consequently we can't have cheap broom travel. We have to send out one or two expeditions each year to buy these materials with gold which we manufacture from the few resources this land does have. To pay for some of this we have high rates of tax and the cost of owning and running a broom is very high. For a long time we have looked for ways of making broom travel cheaper. Anybody with enough money to gamble, and that usually means the faerie, has sunk it into research. This hasn't paid off very well."

"Do you mean that you have been looking for cheap travel all this time and you didn't tell me?"

"Well we didn't think it would be necessary to tell a sorcerer of your power. We thought things like that would be obvious. Anyway, now that you've produced this secret it is very important that we have access to it. It could transform our economy."

"But I've told you once. I've given it to the trolls to make them go away."

"Well you will just have to get it back from them. After all you are the sorcerer."

"But Axel, it's not that easy. If you started a large fire in the forest and somebody insisted that you save one tree, which had already been burned, could you do it?"

"If you put it like that, no, I couldn't, but there must be something you can do."

"I don't know Axel. I shall have to think about it. There are several approaches I could explore but they would all take time which we don't have much of. And I can't be certain they would work.

"We have to try Miko. Lutetia, for one, will commit murder if we don't. If this story ever gets out to the people we could all be struck by lightning."

"Okay," Mike sighed, "When the others get back I'll tell them where we stand and what we may be able to do, but I don't think they will like the alternatives left open to them."

Educating Miko

When the members of the committee returned Mike was pleased to see that they seemed to have forgotten all idea of his having sold out to the trolls. They were now convinced that he was too simple to be that devious. As soon as they were all settled with a drink Mike began, before they could raise more questions. He started by telling them that he finally understood the point they had been making thanks to Axel's explanations. Once he had them believing that he went on to the next stage of his plan. He first asked the committee members individually if they felt sure they could speak with authority for their Guild.

"You see," he continued, "I may need you to agree to things at short notice and I can't have you changing your mind afterward or the spells would stop working."

The committee all said "yes" individually and communally.

"In that case," Mike continued, before he could be interrupted, "I will tell you what I have in mind. It is not easy and it could be quite dangerous but I think I can do it with your help."

He called for another drink, allowing the suspense to build up.

"As I see it the problem is this. You need the secret that I have sorcered up for the trolls. Because of the way I have put the spell together you can't have it, The trolls can't give it to you and there is not time to take it apart before the trolls leave this land,"

Everyone sat round the table nodding vigorously and frowning.

"Well the simplest thing to do would be to ask the trolls to delay their departure until I can do something to change the spell." This brought fourth a burst of comments from around the table.

"We couldn't do that."

"Why not?"

"The trolls would never do anything we asked them."

"Who says? Anyway, we'll make them."

"How?"

The questions and answers flowed quickly around the group doing little to solve the problem but helping Mike a lot by demonstrating the difficulty of the task. The chatter was interrupted by Mike shouting.

"It seems to be the general opinion that we will have too many problems in trying to convince the trolls by asking." The chatter died down. "I think we may be able to accomplish the same thing by trickery. That is by making them think it is in their interest to stay." There was a general buzz of agreement to this.

"There are still some problems though," Mike continued. "As I told you I have put a spell on them making them want to leave, I cannot reverse this unless they can stay here in safety."

"That's no problem Miko. I can pull all the dwarves off them now. I only have to tell them to stop and they'll start fighting among themselves until they're too tired to attack Southend."

"Well that takes care of that. The next problem is how to trick them into staying." The whole group thought about that for a while before anybody replied. It was Axel who ultimately broke the silence.

"The only way to get the trolls to stay is to make them think that we can prevent them from leaving."

"I'm not sure that would make any difference considering the spell I've put on them."

"Well there must be something we can do. You mentioned some other possibilities earlier on, what were they?"

"Well," said Mike slowly, letting everybody catch the uncertainty in his voice, "I think I could remove part of the spell. That part which makes the trolls want to leave this land at any cost. The only problem is that, if I do that the trolls will probably want to invade Midland again."

"That's alright Miko. We'll just set the dwarves on them again."

"No Bandor. That won't do. You still wouldn't have the secret of the ship then."

After Miko said that the group fell back to muttering and murmuring around the table. Nobody had yet come up with the suggestion that Mike was hoping for. He continued to bait his trap.

"You see, what we need is a way of keeping the trolls around for at least thirty days so that I can work on them without the threat of being killed when I'm half way through removing the spell,"

It was, of course, Lutetia who bridged the gap for him.

"Wait a minute," she said. "What would happen if they invaded Midland, and we didn't retaliate?"

"Of course we'd retaliate," said Bandor

"But what if we didn't?"

"I just told you we would."

Lutetia was beginning to lose patience,
"Just for a moment, Bandor, suppose that we didn't."
"You're getting as bad as Miko."
Esmeralda spoke for the first time.
"I think I see what Lutetia is getting at. If we did not retaliate then Miko would have time and peace to sort out the spells for us."
"But we always thump the trolls when they invade us." insisted Bandor. "If we stop now they will think we are weak and then we'll never be rid of them."
"We don't know that," said Leander joining the cause, "Because we don't know what they would do if we didn't fight them."
"But can't you see? They'd do all the unspeakable things we normally prevent them from doing by fighting."
"What unspeakable things Bandor?"
"Things.. so unspeakable.. that I can't bring myself to mention them in front of ladies."
At this the meeting broke up in uproar. Mike sat quietly in his seat watching the seed he had planted growing and developing in their minds. The main supporters of Lutetia's ideas were Esmeralda and Leander. The main dissenters were Bandor and Axel. The rest supported whoever happened to be speaking at the time. After ten minutes of free for all argument Mike decided it was time to interrupt.
"It seems to me," he shouted, "that the idea Lutetia is putting forward is a simple and rather elegant solution to the problem. I remove the troll's compulsion to leave the country and let them invade Midland. You do nothing to prevent them from invading you for five weeks and in that time I will change the spell to let you have the secret of the ships."
This met with cries of both "Yes" and "No" in equal volume.

"Now," Mike continued, "Axel has said that you have spent so long at war with the trolls that the dwarves might be unable to stop themselves from attacking the trolls on sight. Bandor seems to agree with this and be a shining example of what Axel is talking about."

This was also greeted with cries of "Yes" and "No".

"Suppose then, that we do two more things, Suppose we allow that the trolls may be attacked at the first sign of unspeakable deeds. And also suppose that I use the intervening time period not only to change the spells I have already cast but find a new one which will make the trolls stay out of Midland forever."

This was met with a renewed buzz of discussion. Mike did not join in because he could see things developing the way he wanted. After a further fifteen minutes the group had come up with a list of points on which Mike needed to comment. Axel put the questions to him.

"Firstly Miko we would all like to know how confident you feel about your ability to accomplish these things."

"Axel, I am the greatest sorcerer in the land. You might be able to find another who is as great but I doubt it. If I say I can do it, then I can so do. On the other hand I have cut myself rather tight for time. I could use another three weeks. Say eight in all."

"Secondly, what about completing the spells if the trolls begin these unspeakable deeds, or, more realistically, if the dwarves can't keep their hands off the nearest band of passing trolls."

"That is much more of a problem. I suggest that Bandor let it be known that anyone who attacks a troll without a good reason will have to answer to me personally. And then I propose that Bandor, you draw up a list of vile and unspeakable acts for which a troll can be arrested. If you pass that out to your dwarves they can then keep their eyes open for the trolls in the commission of those acts," As he finished saying this Bandor began to scribble furiously on a large pad. Mike looked forward to reading the list.

One by one Mike dealt with the objections and problems raised by the committee. It was late in the night when the group rose from the table satisfied that they had an action plan.

For the next two days Mike worked hard and long hours. He had the help of Axel and many of the students who were all keen to see the working of a live sorcerer. Other members of the committee were involved in other tasks which Mike had set them. The only person not involved was Esmeralda who seemed to be avoiding any contact with Mike at all. At the end of the second day Mike was ready to put the last part of his plan into action. He knew it would take a long time and require a lot of his attention, He decided to sort Esmeralda out before he began.

He finally found her in the University Library. She was pouring over books that meant very little to Mike and she was surrounded by handwritten notes. When he found her he was very stern.

"Esmeralda, you have to come and assist me. You or Axel are the only ones who could handle this job for me."

"Yes Miko."

Mike was stunned. She did not seem to react at all. It was rather like talking to a tree.

He led her from the library down to the Rover. Once in it he drove them both out of the city to a group of trees enclosing a small field. He pulled up in the field and watched Esmeralda's face as she saw what was there.

"Miko," she breathed, "Its...its wonderful. What is it?" Suddenly her eyes were full of the fire Mike recalled from the past.

"It's the first part of my spell for the trolls"

"But what does it do." Her pretty witches face was full of wonder and excitement.

"Its a ballista. We are going to take it to the trolls and use it to break the spell I have put on them."

"How will it do that Miko?"

Mike pointed to a wooden hut which had been quickly put up on the other side of the field .

"Watch that building," he said. As Esmeralda watched Mike gathered all the others present and, once they were clear, released the large catapult. A one hundred pound stone flew gracefully through the air and fell on the roof of the hut which collapsed immediately. Everybody cheered and Esmeralda was completely entranced. It was the first time Mike had seen her really happy since his return.

"Tomorrow," he whispered, "you and I are going to take that to Southend."

At noon the following day Mike, with Esmeralda and Axel in the Rover, pulled the ballista through the troll gate and into Southend. They drove swiftly over the unmade roads that led to Monolith. They passed through the capital city, which was completely deserted and out the other side on the road to the coast. There were very few trolls in evidence along the way and those that were paid no attention to the strangers. As they approached the coast they passed large piles of cut timber that were being prepared by a few trolls but they found no evidence of real industry until they reached the coastline itself.

Axel and Esmeralda were astounded by the sight that greeted them. There were countless trolls who, ignoring the guildsmen, rushed around furiously attending tasks which were beyond the ken of the strangers. In the water a huge structure was taking shape. Trolls carried pieces of timber, both large and small, to and from the structure. Miko pointed to it and said, "That is a ship."

Axel and Esmeralda stared.

"What are we going to do now Miko?" asked Axel.

"We are going to find Bellman and tell him some lies."

Mike left the others standing by the Rover and went off to find the leader of the trolls. He returned with him ten minutes later. Between them the three representatives of the Guilds persuaded Bellman that the ballista should be set up about two hundred yards from where the ship was being built. Surprisingly Bellman had no objections. With the aid of a few trolls Mike maneuvered the catapult into position then he loaded it and in full view of everybody, fired it at the ship. By good fortune, or so it seemed to Esmeralda and Axel, there were no trolls working on the structure at the precise moment that Mike fired the device. As the structure began to crumble into the sea Mike hurriedly spoke to Axel and Esmeralda.

"Once we have established that the ship is broken you have to get back to Midland as quickly as possible to get things in motion. I'll stay here and try to delay the trolls as much as possible. I think I may have trouble delaying them more than a day or so but I'll see what I can do while I'm working on the new spells."

His two companions watched the last of the huge structure slide gracefully into the sea and Miko spent most of his time praying that neither of them had been able to observe closely the size or shape of the ship. As the last of the timbers hit the water Axel and Esmeralda smiled at each other and disappeared. Miko was left looking at Bellman.

"Well," Mike said to the troll, "that didn't go too badly did it?"

"If you say so Miko. I hope that thing we built looked enough like a huge ship for your purpose"

"I think it served its purpose very well Bellman. Now it's up to you and your trolls. You have a big selling job to do."   The sorcerer and the troll smiled at each other and walked away chatting

One week later, to the day, Mike drove back into Westown. He had Bellman in the Rover with him and they drove straight to the University. Although a few heads turned to stare as they walked through the school corridors, Mike was pleasantly surprised by the apparent peace in the town. Axel, when they located him, treated the troll leader with great charm and respect and Bandor even managed a fifteen minute meeting without one threatening action. It became clear to Mike that the Guild Committee had done a very good job of persuading the folk of Midland, including themselves, of the short term acceptability of trolls.

Mike explained to the Guildsman that he had managed to undo the first part of his spell compelling the trolls to leave the land within ten days and that the Guilds should expect the trolls to reappear within a couple of days,

There was an element of ritual to the way the news was accepted but Mike just continued to treat the Guildsmen and troll alike with confidence and assurance that all would work out well for both of them. Each, in their turn felt assured that they were exclusively in Mike's confidence and was prepared to let him get on with his plans.

For three weeks Mike traveled around the land collecting bits and pieces of material and forming them into strange shapes.

In truth he had no idea what he was looking for when he began these journeys and constructions but the finished products seemed to be obscure and mystical enough to satisfy everybody that he was doing a good job of sorcering. During this period the trolls made their first ever, peaceful appearance in Midland. They traveled in small groups, unarmed, and went out of their way to be courteous to the Guilds folk, particularly the dwarves. They traveled over much of the country from Westown to Millville and made a point of not hurrying. As this was happening Mike spent a lot of time watching to see if his plans would be realized. By the end of the three weeks he was sure they would.

The first people to discover the potential of the trolls were, of course, the faerie. They soon discovered that the trolls were adept traders and negotiators and were in a position to trade a few highly desirable goods. In small corners of the land bargains began to be struck. Initially they were short term in nature but as confidence grew on both sides credit was extended and both the trolls and the Guilds found themselves very tempted to commit themselves to long-term agreements.

For a while Mike thought that his propaganda to both sides had been too good. Everybody was waiting for his miracle. He had to find a way of putting the final, vital spark to the situation he had created with so much care. He chose Lutetia as the medium for this operation.

At a small dinner at the University he presented his final spells to Axel, Bandor and Lutetia. The showpiece of the evening was a model of a ship he had previously asked the trolls to make. After the meal was cleared away and everybody was comfortable Mike began to work the last part of his magic. He spoke softly and had difficulty keeping the excitement from his voice.

"You see, I have achieved your aims. I can now let you have the secret of sailing," With a flourish he produced the model and everybody looked on with awe. He explained the principle very simply. "You can see from this how the spell works. And no matter how big you make this structure it will always float provided there is enough water." His three companions were agog with excitement.

"It's incredible Miko. When are you going to build the first real one? A full size one that is."

Mike looked at them, a puzzled frown on his face.

"I'm not. I've given you the details of the spell. It's up to you to cast it at the size you want to."

"But we can't. We're not sorcerers. You'll have to do it for us Miko,"

Axel's voice had a pleading note in it.

"But Axel, I can't do it on my own. It's a very big spell. If I do it, it will take years. I think I've done my bit by releasing the trolls from their mastery of it. Now it's up to you."

"But look," put in Bandor, "You were going to build them for the trolls weren't you?"

"No. I most certainly was not. I gave them the original spell and they set about building the ship themselves."

"Well if we can't and you can't,,, what use is the spell to us?" asked Axel,

"Hold on," said Lutetia, impatient with the others and their inability to see the obvious. "It sounds as though the only way we are going to get any real value out of this deal is if we get someone else to cast the spells for us. Miko is saying that it's too much for him and that the trolls managed it with some instruction."

"Well we've always suspected the trolls of practising sorcery."

"I know that Axel but we may be able to get something out of this if we go about it the right way."

Mike held his breath and waited. Lutetia continued,

"We know the trolls can cast the spells and I know that they are critically short of broom technology. I think we could work out a deal with some of them so that they would do the actual spell casting if we would help them with brooms. We could even tie in some foodstuff trade with the whole deal to get it off the ground."

"The only trouble with that is that Miko has promised to get the trolls out of the land by the end of next week," said Bandor with a perplexed look on his face.

"What about that Miko? Have you completed the spell which will banish the trolls?"

"No. Not yet. I think it will take all the time I have available."

"Then we can do it," said Lutetia triumphantly.

"Do what?" asked Axel and Bandor together.

"Make a deal with the trolls. Miko can hold up the spell to banish them."

The meeting immediately turned into an argument. Mike did not join in at all, leaving it to Lutetia and economics to convince the other two that it was a good idea. She succeeded within five minutes. Even Bandor became enthusiastic about the idea once the real impact of the scheme was made clear to him.

"Wait a minute," Mike interrupted their discussion, "are you telling me that I don't have to continue my spells to banish the trolls, because if you are I want to hear it from the whole of the Guild committee. I've been messed about enough by you lot not explaining things or changing your minds. I'm not going to do a thing until you have all agreed on this decision!"

Lutetia and her co-conspirators went into a huddle. When they came out of it Axel said

"Miko, we would like to think about this. When would be the last moment we could ask you not to cast the spell?"

Mike gave them two days. He hoped it was enough.

Two days later Mike sat with the full committee. The meeting had been called by Axel. Mike had protested at being dragged away from his sorcery but had consented to come if they kept it short. Axel began the meeting without his usual preamble.

"We have called this meeting to bring you all up to date with what is happening. Then we would to put some proposals to you for a vote. As you recall we asked Miko to get the secret of the ship released from his spell on the trolls so that we could get some economic benefit from it. Well he has done this but there are a few problems. The main one is that we need somebody to cast the spells now that we have the details of them. Here in Midland we have no skills in sorcery, save those of Miko here, but by asking a few questions we have found that the trolls have enough skills to be able to cast the spells under our, or Miko's, direction."

There was a short pause while people thought about this and shuffled their feet. Axel continued,

"It looks as though we may have to enlist the aid of the trolls if we are going to reap any substantial benefit from this situation."

Another pause. More shuffling.

"The only way we can do this is to ask Miko not to complete his spell to banish the trolls." The last comment met with a gasp and a number of smiles. Esmeralda was the first to recover.

"Do you mean that after all the work Miko has done and the risks he has taken, you don't want him to finish his job?"

"Er...Yes. That's what we mean."

Before Esmeralda could reply Irving interrupted.

"Well I for one think it's a jolly fine idea. I've found out a lot about the trolls in the past six weeks. They're not at all the bloodthirsty chaps we had always thought they were. They are very nice and I get on well with them."

"They also buy a lot of your fishing rods," added Pallisy with a smirk.

Axel brought the meeting back to order before it could degenerate.

"The thing we want to know now is, does anybody feel that the trolls must go at any price"

Nobody did.

"Good," continued Axel, "because Lutetia and Bandor have been negotiating with some of the trolls for the last two days and have reached an agreement which ensures that the trolls will build ships for us, to our specification, and we will pay them in brooms."

He paused for a moment and crossed the room to the door. He opened it and outside stood two trolls.

"For those of you who have not met them these two trolls are Bellman and Landsman. They can speak for the trolls in much the same way that we speak for the Guilds. They are here to finalise the agreement by formally signing it."

"It's all very well us signing it," said Esmeralda, "but what are we going to do about the dwarves. If the trolls don't disappear will the dwarves do something dangerous?"

Bellman and Landsman looked embarrassed. Axel stood up smiling.

"Yes. You might think that would be the case but some very strange things have been happening lately. For the first time the dwarves have found a peer group. That is people who are physically tough, self sufficient and afraid of nothing. As much as I hate to say it the dwarf in the street now gets on better with the trolls than he does with many of the Guild folk."

Esmeralda burst out laughing at this and Mike smiled at seeing her happy.

There was a short silence while Axel waited for further comment which did not come.

"If that is all then I suggest we sign this agreement."

As the individuals round the table signed the agreement Mike heaved a large metaphorical sigh of relief.

"Do I understand that you no longer wish me to continue with the second half of my spells then?"

"Poor Miko," said Axel. "You're not really cut out for the political side of life. I suggest that you stop work now and let us, with our greater experience, handle the situation."

Epilogue

Once the news of the agreement was announced deals with the trolls sprang up all over the land. Within a week the disappearance of the trolls was a forgotten threat which would have wrought economic havoc had it occurred. The mood of optimism which ran through all the people was apparent from the number of spontaneous celebrations that sprang up and lasted until the ale ran out. One of the more magnificent of these celebration parties was that organised by the Guilds negotiating committee. It included the whole of the Southend Planning Authority and many of the more active traders among the trolls and the Guilds. There was a great deal of preparation for it and food and drink to cater for all tastes was provided. It was held in the open air in the square by which Mike had entered the University.

Mike wandered around the party chatting idly with people. He somehow could not bring himself to enjoy it. The success of his work was apparent from the conversations he overheard. Plans were being made for all sorts of further trade agreements and each group was learning a lot from the other. It seemed to Mike that he had no place in the new order that was arising. At the back of his mind he was also worried about getting back to the real world. Although he had accepted the reality of his surroundings he still did not understand where he was or how he could return to his own time and place. He found the crowd and the party rather overpowering and prepared to leave.

As he stepped into the corridor leading to his room he felt a tap on his shoulder and turned to find Esmeralda facing him.

"You can't leave now Miko. The party is just beginning."

"Well I never did go much on parties Esmeralda."

"Okay, but you must have one drink with me before you go." Mike could not refuse such a gracious request and the beautiful witch slipped away to procure two drinks. When she returned they stood in the silent corridor talking.

Somehow they never discussed the things Mike had done in his three month stay in Midland. They talked about Mike's home in Ireland, his experience in the USA and his work in Canada. Esmeralda was interested in the places Mike talked about and he found himself describing them in more and more detail, along with his lifestyle and the differences between his own world and Midland.

"I think, Miko, that you should take me to this place and show it to me,"

"That's a nice idea, but unfortunately I don't know how I got here or how to get back."

"Oh that's no problem. I worked with Axel on the incantations to get you here and in the last few weeks I have done a lot of work on the kinetics of the two worlds. Now I have set things up such that you can go back and fourth between the two in much the same way that you would around Midland."

"You seem to forget that I can't do that trick of yours. I have to travel by Rover."

"That's no problem either. Hold on to my hands."

Mike held her warm hands and there was a sudden funny, unfamiliar feeling in his stomach. He found himself and Esmeralda sitting in the Rover."

"Why didn't you do that when I first arrived here instead of making me drive all those miles?" he gasped.

"Well for one thing I didn't have the power then, secondly I was very tired and thirdly... it was rather nice once I was cuddled up against you like this." She moved closer to him and he automatically put his arm round her shoulder. "That's nice," she said, "But perhaps I was a little closer."

Well I'll never be able to drive back to Ireland like this." Mike laughed softly. "I can't concentrate on driving."

"Don't try," whispered Esmeralda. Just close your eyes and think about the place you would most like to be."

Mike closed his eyes and thought briefly about a small village in the southwest of Ireland. He thought of the view over the estuary and how it would look to Esmeralda in the moonlight. Suddenly he felt again that unfamiliar feeling in his stomach and he knew that when he opened his eyes they would be back home in the village of his birth.

www.ingramcontent.com/pod-product-compliance
Lightning Source LLC
Chambersburg PA
CBHW020538160726
47991CB00002B/493